A HANDFUL OF
HORRiD
HENRY

Francesca Simon is an American who lives
in London with her English husband and
her son. She grew up in California, was
educated at Yale and Oxford Universities,
and was a freelance journalist, writing theatre
and restaurant reviews for some years. She
is now a very successful writer of children's
books, ranging from picture books to young
fiction.

Also by Francesca Simon

Horris Henry's Nits
Horrid Henry Gets Rich Quick
(previously published as *Horrid Henry Strikes it Rich*)
Horrid Henry's Haunted House
Horrid Henry and the Mummy's Curse
Horrid Henry's Revenge
Horrid Henry and the Bogey Babysitter
Horrid Henry's Stinkbomb
Horrid Henry's Underpants
Horrid Henry Meets the Queen
Horrid Henry and the Mega-Mean Time Machine
Horrid Henry and the Football Fiend
Horrid Henry's Christmas Cracker

Horrid Henry's Big Bad Book
Horrid Henry's Wicked Ways
Horrid Henry's Evil Enemies
Horrid Henry's Joke Book

Don't Cook Cinderella
Helping Hercules

and for younger readers
Don't Be Horrid, Henry
Illustrated by Kevin McAleenan
The Topsy-Turvies
Illustrated by Emily Bolam

A HANDFUL OF
HORRiD
HENRY

Francesca Simon
Illustrated by Tony Ross

Orion
Children's Books

First published in Great Britain in 2000
by Orion Children's Books
a division of the Orion Publishing Group Ltd
Orion House
5 Upper St Martin's Lane
London WC2H 9EA

15 17 19 20 18 16 14

ISBN-10 1 85881 847 8
ISBN-13 978 1 85881 847 4

The Orion Publishing Group's policy is to use papers that
are natural, renewable and recyclable products and
made from wood grown in sustainable forests. The logging
and manufacturing processes are expected to conform to
the environmental regulations of the country of origin.

A catalogue record for this book
is available from the British Library

Printed in Great Britain
by Clays Ltd, St Ives plc

www.orionbooks.co.uk

CONTENTS

HORRID
HENRY

For Joshua and his friends —
Dominic, Eleanor, Freddie, Harry,
Joe, Robbie, and Toby,
with love

CONTENTS

1

HORRID HENRY'S PERFECT DAY

Henry was horrid.

Everyone said so, even his mother.

Henry threw food, Henry snatched, Henry pushed and shoved and pinched. Even his teddy avoided him when possible.

His parents despaired.

"What are we going to do about that horrid boy?" sighed Mum.

"How did two people as nice as us have such a horrid child?" sighed Dad.

When Horrid Henry's parents took Henry to school they walked behind him and pretended he was not theirs.

Children pointed at Henry and whispered to their parents, "That's Horrid Henry."

"He's the boy who threw my jacket in the mud."

"He's the boy who squashed Billy's beetle."

"He's the boy who . . ." Fill in whatever terrible deed you like. Horrid Henry was sure to have done it.

Horrid Henry had
a younger brother.
His name was
Perfect Peter.

Perfect Peter
always said "Please"
and "Thank you".
Perfect Peter loved
vegetables.

Perfect Peter
always used a hankie
and never, ever
picked his nose.

"Why can't you
be perfect like
Peter?" said Henry's
mum every day.

13

As usual, Henry pretended not to hear. He continued melting Peter's crayons on the radiator.

But Horrid Henry started to think.

"What if *I* were perfect?" thought Henry. "I wonder what would happen."

When Henry woke the next morning, he did not wake Peter by pouring water on Peter's head.

Peter did not scream.

This meant Henry's parents overslept and Henry and Peter were late for Cubs.

Henry was very happy.

Peter was very sad to be late for Cubs.

But because he was perfect, Peter did not whine or complain.

On the way to Cubs Henry did not squabble with Peter over who sat in front. He did not pinch Peter and he did not shove Peter.

Back home, when Perfect Peter built a castle, Henry did not knock it down. Instead, Henry sat on the sofa and read a book.

Mum and Dad ran into the room.

"It's awfully quiet in here," said Mum. "Are you being horrid, Henry?"

"No," said Henry.

"Peter, is Henry knocking your castle down?"

Peter longed to say "yes". But that would be a lie.

"No," said Peter.

He wondered why Henry was behaving so strangely.

"What are you doing, Henry?" said Dad.

"Reading a wonderful story about some super mice," said Henry.

Dad had never seen Henry read a book before. He checked to see if a comic was hidden inside.

There was no comic. Henry was actually reading a book.

"Hmmmm," said Dad.

It was almost time for dinner. Henry was hungry and went into the kitchen where Dad was cooking.

But instead of shouting, "I'm starving! Where's my food?" Henry said, "Dad, you look tired. Can I help get supper ready?"

"Don't be horrid, Henry," said Dad, pouring peas into boiling water. Then he stopped.

"What did you say, Henry?" asked Dad.

"Can *I* help, Dad?" said Perfect Peter.

"I asked if you needed any help," said Henry.

"I asked first," said Peter.

"Henry will just make a mess," said Dad. "Peter, would you peel the carrots while I sit down for a moment?"

19

"Of course," said
Perfect Peter.

Peter washed his
spotless hands.

Peter put on his
spotless apron.

Peter rolled up his
spotless sleeves.

Peter waited for
Henry to snatch the
peeler.

But Henry laid the table instead.

Mum came into the kitchen.

"Smells good," she said. "Thank you, darling Peter, for laying the table. What a good boy you are."

Peter did not say anything.

"I laid the table, Mum," said Henry.

Mum stared at him.

"You?" said Mum.

"Me," said Henry.

"Why?" said Mum.

Henry smiled.

"To be helpful," he said.

"You've done something horrid, haven't you, Henry?" said Dad.

"No," said Henry. He tried to look sweet.

"I'll lay the table tomorrow," said Perfect Peter.

"Thank you, angel," said Mum.

"Dinner is ready," said Dad.

The family sat down at the table.

Dinner was spaghetti and meatballs with peas and carrots.

Henry ate his dinner with his knife and fork and spoon.

He did not throw peas at Peter and he did not slurp.

He did not chew with his mouth open and he did not slouch.

"Sit properly, Henry," said Dad.

"I am sitting properly," said Henry.

Dad looked up from his plate. He looked surprised.

"So you are," he said.

Perfect Peter could not eat. Why wasn't Henry throwing peas at him?

Peter's hand reached slowly for a pea.

When no one was looking, he flicked the pea at Henry.

"Ouch," said Henry.

"Don't be horrid, Henry," said Mum.

Henry reached for a fistful of peas. Then Henry remembered he was being perfect and stopped.

Peter smiled and waited. But no peas bopped him on the head.

Perfect Peter did not understand. Where was the foot that always kicked him under the table?

Slowly, Peter stretched out his foot and kicked Henry.

"OUCH," said Henry.

"Don't be horrid, Henry," said Dad.

"But I . . ." said Henry, then stopped.

Henry's foot wanted to kick Perfect Peter round the block. Then Henry remembered he was being perfect and continued to eat.

"You're very quiet tonight, Henry," said Dad.

"The better to enjoy my lovely dinner," said Henry.

"Henry, where are your peas and carrots?" asked Mum.

"I ate them," said Henry. "They were delicious."

Mum looked on the floor. She looked under Henry's chair. She looked under his plate.

"You ate your peas and carrots?"
said Mum slowly. She felt Henry's
forehead.

"Are you feeling all right, Henry?"

"Yeah," said Horrid Henry. "I'm
fine, thank you for asking," he added
quickly.

Mum and Dad looked at each other. What was going on?

Then they looked at Henry.

"Henry, come here and let me give you a big kiss," said Mum. "You are a wonderful boy. Would you like a piece of fudge cake?"

Peter interrupted.

"No cake for me, thank you," said Peter. "I would rather have more vegetables."

Henry let himself be kissed. Oh my, it was hard work being perfect.

He smiled sweetly at Peter.

"I would love some cake, thank you," said Henry.

Perfect Peter could stand it no longer. He picked up his plate and aimed at Henry.

Then Peter threw the spaghetti.

Henry ducked.

SPLAT!

Spaghetti landed on Mum's head. Tomato sauce trickled down her neck and down her new yellow fuzzy jumper.

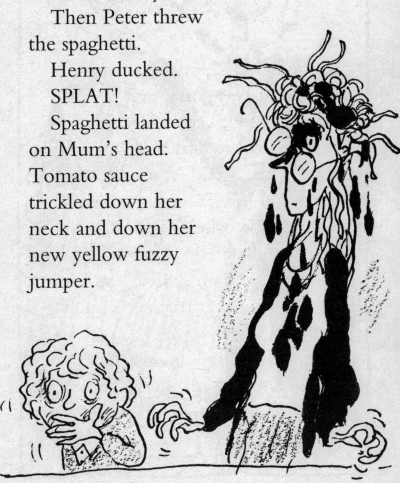

"PETER!!!!" yelled Mum and Dad.

"YOU HORRID BOY!" yelled Mum.

"GO TO YOUR ROOM!!" yelled Dad.

Perfect Peter burst into tears and ran to his room.

Mum wiped spaghetti off her face. She looked very funny.

Henry tried not to laugh. He squeezed his lips together tightly.

But it was no use. I am sorry to say that he could not stop a laugh escaping.

"It's not funny!" shouted Dad.

"Go to your room!" shouted Mum.

But Henry didn't care.

Who would have thought being perfect would be such fun?

2

·······································

HORRID HENRY'S DANCE CLASS

Stomp Stomp Stomp Stomp Stomp Stomp Stomp.

Horrid Henry was practising his elephant dance.

Tap Tap Tap Tap Tap Tap Tap Tap.

Perfect Peter was practising his raindrop dance.

Peter was practising being a raindrop for his dance class show.

Henry was also supposed to be practising being a raindrop.

But Henry did not want to be a raindrop. He did not want to be a tomato, a string bean, or a banana either.

Stomp Stomp Stomp went Henry's heavy boots.

Tap Tap Tap went Peter's tap shoes.

"You're doing it wrong, Henry," said Peter.

"No I'm not," said Henry.

"You are too," said Peter. "We're supposed to be raindrops."

Stomp Stomp Stomp went Henry's boots. He was an elephant smashing his way through the jungle, trampling on everyone who stood in his way.

"I can't concentrate with you stomping," said Peter. "And I have to practise my solo."

"Who cares?" screamed Horrid Henry. "I hate dancing, I hate dance class, and most of all, I hate you!"

This was not entirely true. Horrid Henry loved dancing. Henry danced in his bedroom. Henry danced up and down the stairs. Henry danced on the new sofa and on the kitchen table.

What Henry hated was having to dance with other children.

"Couldn't I go to karate instead?" asked Henry every Saturday.

"No," said Mum. "Too violent."

"Judo?" said Henry.

"N–O spells no," said Dad.

So every Saturday morning at 9.45 a.m., Henry and Peter's father drove them to Miss Impatience Tutu's Dance Studio.

Miss Impatience Tutu was skinny and bony. She had long stringy grey hair. Her nose was sharp. Her elbows were pointy. Her knees were knobbly. No one had ever seen her smile.

Perhaps this was because Impatience Tutu hated teaching.

Impatience Tutu hated noise.

Impatience Tutu hated children.

But most of all Impatience Tutu hated Horrid Henry.

This was not surprising. When Miss

Tutu shouted, "Class, lift your left legs," eleven left legs lifted. One right leg sagged to the floor.

When Miss Tutu screamed, "Heel, toe, heel, toe," eleven dainty feet tapped away. One clumpy foot stomped toe, heel, toe, heel.

When Miss Tutu bellowed, "Class, skip to your right," eleven bodies turned to the right. One body galumphed to the left.

Naturally, no one wanted to dance with Henry. Or indeed, anywhere near Henry. Today's class, unfortunately, was no different.

"Miss Tutu, Henry is treading on my toes," said Jumpy Jeffrey.

"Miss Tutu, Henry is kicking my legs," said Lazy Linda.

"Miss Tutu, Henry is bumping me," said Vain Violet.

"HENRY!" screeched Miss Tutu.

"Yeah," said Henry.

"I am a patient woman, and you are trying my patience to the limit," hissed Miss Tutu. "Any more bad behaviour and you will be very sorry."

"What will happen?" asked Horrid Henry eagerly.

Miss Tutu stood very tall. She took a long, bony finger and dragged it slowly across her throat.

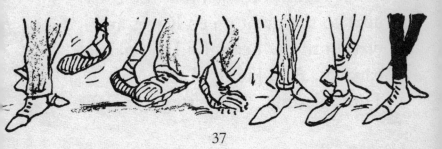

Henry decided that he would rather live to do battle another day. He stood on the side, gnashing his teeth, pretending he was an enormous crocodile about to gobble up Miss Tutu.

"This is our final rehearsal before the show," barked Miss Tutu. "Everything must be perfect."

Eleven faces stared at Miss Tutu. One face scowled at the floor.

"Tomatoes and beans to the front," ordered Miss Tutu.

"When Miss Thumper plays the music everyone will stretch out their arms to the sky, to kiss the morning hello. Raindrops, stand at the back next to the giant green leaves and wait until the beans find the magic bananas. And Henry," spat Miss Tutu, glaring. "TRY to get it right.

"Positions, everybody. Miss Thumper, the opening music please!" shouted Miss Tutu.

Miss Thumper banged away.

The tomatoes weaved in and out, twirling.

The beans pirouetted.

The bananas pointed their toes and swayed.

The raindrops pitter–patted.

All except one. Henry waved his arms frantically and raced round the room. Then he crashed into the beans.

"HENRY!" screeched Miss Tutu.

"Yeah," scowled Henry.

"Sit in the corner!"

Henry was delighted. He sat in the corner and made horrible rude faces while Peter did his raindrop solo.

Tap tap tap tap tap tap tap. Tappa tappa tappa tappa tap tap tap. Tappa tip tappa tip tappa tappa tappa tip.

"Was that perfect, Miss Tutu?" asked Peter.

Miss Tutu sighed. "Perfect, Peter, as always," she said, and the corner of her mouth trembled slightly. This was the closest Miss Tutu ever came to smiling.

Then she saw Henry slouching on

the chair. Her mouth drooped back into its normal grim position.

Miss Tutu tugged Henry off the chair. She shoved him to the very back of the stage, behind the other raindrops. Then she pushed him behind a giant green leaf.

"Stand there!" shouted Miss Tutu.

"But no one will see me here," said Henry.

"Precisely," said Miss Tutu.

It was showtime.

The curtain was about to rise.

The children stood quietly on stage.

Perfect Peter was so excited he almost bounced up and down. Naturally he controlled himself and stood still.

Horrid Henry was not very
excited.

He did not want to be a raindrop.

And he certainly did not want to be
a raindrop who danced behind a giant
green leaf.

Miss Thumper waddled over to the
piano. She banged on the keys.

The curtain went up.

Henry's mum and dad were in the audience with the other parents. As usual they sat in the back row, in case they had to make a quick getaway.

They smiled and waved at Peter, standing proudly at the front.

"Can you see Henry?" whispered Henry's mum.

Henry's dad squinted at the stage.

A tuft of red hair stuck up behind the green leaf.

"I think that's him behind the leaf," said his father doubtfully.

"I wonder why Henry is hiding," said Mum. "It's not like him to be shy."

"Hmmmm," said Dad.

"Shhh," hissed the parents beside them.

Henry watched the tomatoes and beans searching on tiptoe for the magic bananas.

I'm not staying back here, he thought, and pushed his way through the raindrops.

"Stop pushing, Henry!" hissed Lazy Linda.

Henry pushed harder, then did a few pitter-pats with the other raindrops.

Miss Tutu stretched out a bony arm and yanked Henry back behind the scenery.

Who wants to be a raindrop anyway, thought Henry. I can do what I like hidden here.

The tomatoes weaved in and out, twirling.

The beans pirouetted.

The bananas pointed their toes and swayed.

The raindrops pitter-patted.

Henry flapped his arms and pretended he was a *pterodactyl* about to pounce on Miss Tutu.

Round and round he flew, homing in on his prey.

Perfect Peter stepped to the front and began his solo.

47

Tap Tap Tap Tap Tap Tap – CRASH!

One giant green leaf fell on top of the raindrops, knocking them over.

The raindrops collided with the tomatoes.

The tomatoes smashed into the string beans.

The string beans bumped into the bananas.

Perfect Peter turned his head to see what was happening and danced off the stage into the front row.

Miss Tutu fainted.

The only person still standing on stage was Henry.

Stomp Stomp Stomp Stomp Stomp Stomp Stomp.

Henry did his
elephant dance.
Boom Boom
Boom Boom Boom
Boom Boom.
Henry did his
wild buffalo dance.

Peter tried to scramble back on stage.

The curtain fell.

There was a long silence, then Henry's parents clapped.

No one else did, so Henry's parents stopped.

All the other parents ran up to Miss Tutu and started shouting.

"I don't see why that horrid boy should have had such a long solo while all Linda did was lie on the floor," yelled one mother.

"My Jeffrey is a much better dancer than that boy," shouted another. "He should have done the solo."

"I didn't know you taught modern dance, Miss Tutu," said Violet's mother. "Come, Violet," she added, sweeping from the room.

"HENRY!!" screeched Miss Tutu. "Leave my dance studio at once!"

"Whoopee!" shouted Henry. He knew that next Saturday he would be at karate class at last.

3

....

HORRID HENRY AND MOODY MARGARET

"I'm Captain Hook!"

"No, I'm Captain Hook!"

"I'm Captain Hook," said Horrid Henry.

"I'm Captain Hook," said Moody Margaret.

They glared at each other.

"It's *my* hook," said Moody Margaret.

Moody Margaret lived next door.

She did not like Horrid
Henry, and Horrid
Henry did not like
her. But when Rude
Ralph was busy, Clever
Clare had flu, and Sour
Susan was her enemy,
Margaret would jump
over the wall to play
with Henry.

"Actually, it's my turn to be Hook
now," said Perfect Peter. "I've been
the prisoner for such a long time."

"Prisoner, be quiet!" said Henry.

"Prisoner, walk the plank!" said
Margaret.

"But I've walked it fourteen times
already," said Peter. "Please can I be
Hook now?"

"No, by thunder!" said Moody
Margaret. "Now out of my way,

54

worm!" And she swashbuckled across
the deck, waving her hook and
clutching her sword and dagger.

Margaret had eyepatches and skulls
and crossbones and plumed hats and
cutlasses and sabres and snickersnees.

Henry had a stick.

This was why Henry played with
Margaret.

But Henry had to do terrible things
before playing with Margaret's

swords. Sometimes he had to sit and wait while she read a book. Sometimes he had to play "Mums and Dads" with her. Worst of all (please don't tell anyone), sometimes he had to be the baby.

Henry never knew what Margaret would do.

When he put a spider on her arm, Margaret laughed.

When he pulled her hair, Margaret pulled his harder.

When Henry screamed, Margaret would scream louder. Or she would sing. Or pretend not to hear.

Sometimes Margaret was fun. But most of the time she was a moody old grouch.

"I won't play if I can't be Hook," said Horrid Henry.

Margaret thought for a moment.

"We can both be Captain Hook," she said.

"But we only have one hook," said Henry.

"Which I haven't played with yet," said Peter.

"BE QUIET, prisoner!" shouted Margaret. "Mr Smee, take him to jail."

"No," said Henry.

"You will get your reward, Mr Smee," said the Captain, waving her hook.

Mr Smee dragged the prisoner to the jail.

"If you're very quiet, prisoner, then you will be freed and you can be a pirate, too," said Captain Hook.

"Now give me the hook," said Mr Smee.

The Captain reluctantly handed it over.

"Now I'm Captain Hook and you're Mr Smee," shouted Henry. "I order everyone to walk the plank!"

"I'm sick of playing pirates," said Margaret. "Let's play something else."

Henry was furious. That was just like Moody Margaret.

"Well, I'm playing pirates," said
Henry.

"Well I'm not," said Margaret.
"Give me back my hook."

"No," said Henry.

Moody Margaret
opened her mouth
and screamed. Once
Margaret started
screaming she could
go on and on and
on.

Henry gave her
the hook.

Margaret smiled.

"I'm hungry,"
she said. "Got
anything good to
eat?"

Henry had three bags of crisps and
seven chocolate biscuits hidden in his

room, but he certainly wasn't going to share them with Margaret.

'You can have a radish," said Henry.

"What else?" said Margaret.

"A carrot," said Henry.

"What else?" said Margaret.

"Glop," said Henry.

"What's Glop?"

"Something special that only I can make," said Henry.

"What's in it? asked Margaret.

"That's a secret," said Henry.

"I bet it's yucky," said Margaret.

"Of course it's yucky," said Henry.

"I can make the yuckiest Glop of all," said Margaret.

"That's because you don't know anything. No one can make yuckier Glop than I can."

"I dare you to eat Glop," said Margaret.

"I double dare you back," said Henry. "Dares go first."

Margaret stood up very straight.

"All right," said Margaret. "Glop starts with snails and worms."

And she started poking under the bushes.

"Got one!" she shouted, holding up a fat snail.

"Now for some worms," said Margaret.

She got down on her hands and knees and started digging a hole.

"You can't put anything from outside into Glop," said Henry quickly. "Only stuff in the kitchen."

Margaret looked at Henry.

"I thought we were making Glop," she said.

"We are," said Henry. "My way, because it's *my* house."

Horrid Henry and Moody Margaret went into the gleaming white kitchen. Henry got out two wooden mixing spoons and a giant red bowl.

"I'll start," said Henry. He went to the cupboard and opened the doors wide.

"Porridge!" said Henry. And he poured some into the bowl.

Margaret opened the fridge and

looked inside. She grabbed a small
container.

"Soggy semolina!" shouted
Margaret. Into the bowl it went.

"Coleslaw!"

"Spinach!"

"Coffee!"

"Yoghurt!"

"Flour!"

"Vinegar!"

"Baked beans!"

"Mustard!"

"Peanut butter!"

"Mouldy cheese!"

"Pepper!"

"Rotten oranges!"

"And ketchup!" shouted Henry.
He squirted in the ketchup until the
bottle was empty.

"Now, mix!" said Margaret.

Horrid Henry and Moody
Margaret grabbed hold of their
spoons with both hands. Then they
plunged the spoons into the Glop and
began to stir.

It was hard heavy work.

Faster and faster, harder and harder
they stirred.

There was Glop on the ceiling.
There was Glop on the floor. There
was Glop on the clock, and Glop on
the door. Margaret's hair was covered
in Glop. So was Henry's face.

Margaret looked into the bowl. She
had never seen anything so yucky in
her life.

"It's ready," she said.

Horrid Henry and Moody
Margaret carried the Glop to the
table.

Then they sat down and stared at
the sloppy, slimy, sludgy, sticky,
smelly, gooey, gluey, gummy,
greasy, gloopy Glop.

"Right," said Henry. "Who's
going to eat some first?"

There was a very
long pause.

Henry looked at
Margaret.

Margaret looked
at Henry.

"Me," said
Margaret. "I'm not
scared."

She scooped up a
large spoonful and
stuffed it in her mouth.

Then she
swallowed. Her face
went pink and
purple and green.

"How does it
taste?" said Henry.

"Good," said
Margaret, trying not
to choke.

"Have some more
then," said Henry.

"Your turn first,"
said Margaret.

Henry sat for a moment and looked at the Glop.

"My mum doesn't like me to eat between meals," said Henry.

"HENRY!" hissed Moody Margaret.

Henry took a tiny spoonful.

"More!" said Margaret.

Henry took a tiny bit more. The Glop wobbled lumpily on his spoon. It looked like . . . Henry did not want to think about what it looked like.

He closed his eyes and brought the spoon to his mouth.

"Ummm, yummm," said Henry.

"You didn't eat any," said Margaret. "That's not fair."

She scooped up some Glop and . . .

I dread to think what would have

happened next, if they had not been interrupted.

"Can I come out now?" called a small voice from outside. "It's my turn to be Hook."

Horrid Henry had forgotten all about Perfect Peter.

"OK," shouted Henry.

Peter came to the door.

"I'm hungry," he said.

"Come in, Peter," said Henry sweetly. "Your dinner is on the table."

4

HORRID HENRY'S HOLIDAY

Horrid Henry hated holidays.

Henry's idea of a super holiday was sitting on the sofa eating crisps and watching TV.

Unfortunately, his parents usually had other plans.

Once they took him to see some castles. But there were no castles. There were only piles of stones and broken walls.

"Never again," said Henry.

The next year he had to go to a lot of museums.

"Never again," said Mum and Dad.

Last year they went to the seaside.

"The sun is too hot," Henry whined.

"The water is too cold," Henry whinged.

"The food is yucky," Henry
grumbled.

"The bed is lumpy," Henry
moaned.

This year they decided to try something different.

"We're going camping in France," said Henry's parents.

"Horray!" said Henry.

"You're happy, Henry?" said Mum. Henry had never been happy about any holiday plans before.

"Oh yes," said Henry. Finally, finally, they were doing something good.

Henry knew all about camping from Moody Margaret. Margaret had been camping with her family. They had stayed in a big tent with comfy beds, a fridge, a cooker, a loo, a shower, a heated swimming pool, a disco, and a great big giant TV with fifty-seven channels.

"Oh boy!" said Horrid Henry.

"Bonjour!" said Perfect Peter.

The great day arrived at last. Horrid Henry, Perfect Peter, Mum and Dad boarded the ferry for France.

Henry and Peter had never been on a boat before.

Henry jumped on and off the seats.

Peter did a lovely drawing.

The boat went up and down and up and down.

Henry ran back
and forth between
the aisles.

Peter pasted
stickers in his
notebook.

The boat went up
and down and up
and down.

Henry sat on a
revolving chair and
spun round.

Peter played with
his puppets.

The boat went up
and down and up
and down.

Then Henry and
Peter ate a big
greasy lunch of
sausages and chips

in the café.

The boat went up
and down, and up
and down, and up
and down.

Henry began to
feel queasy.

Peter began to
feel queasy.

Henry's face went
green.

Peter's face went
green.

"I think I'm going to be sick," said
Henry, and threw up all over Mum.

"I think I'm going to be —" said
Peter, and threw up all over Dad.

"Oh no," said Mum.

"Never mind," said Dad. "I just
know this will be our best holiday
ever."

Finally, the boat arrived in France.

After driving and driving and driving they reached the campsite.

It was even better than Henry's dreams. The tents were as big as houses. Henry heard the happy sound of TVs blaring, music playing, and children splashing and shrieking. The sun shone. The sky was blue.

"Wow, this looks great," said Henry.

But the car drove on.

"Stop!" said Henry. "You've gone too far."

"We're not staying in that awful place," said Dad.

They drove on.

"Here's our campsite,' said Dad. "A *real* campsite!"

Henry stared at the bare rocky ground under the cloudy grey sky.

There were three small tents flapping
in the wind. There was a single tap.
There were a few trees. There was
nothing else.

"It's wonderful!" said Mum.

"It's wonderful!" said Peter.

"But where's the TV?" said Henry.

"No TV here, thank goodness,"
said Mum. "We've got books."

"But where are the beds?" said
Henry.

"No beds here, thank goodness,"
said Dad. "We've got sleeping bags."

"But where's the pool?" said
Henry.

"No pool," said Dad. "*We'll* swim
in the river."

"Where's the toilet?" said Peter.
Dad pointed at a distant cubicle.
Three people stood waiting.

"All the way over there?" said Peter. "I'm not complaining," he added quickly.

Mum and Dad unpacked the car. Henry stood and scowled.

"Who wants to help put up the tent?" asked Mum.

"I do!" said Dad.

"I do!" said Peter.

Henry was horrified. "We have to put up our own tent?"

"Of course," said Mum.

"I don't like it here," said Henry.

"I want to go camping in the other place."

"That's not camping," said Dad. "Those tents have beds in them. And loos. And showers. And fridges. And cookers, and TVs. Horrible." Dad shuddered.

"Horrible," said Peter.

"And we have such a lovely snug tent here," said Mum. "Nothing modern — just wooden pegs and poles."

"Well, I want to stay there," said Henry.

"We're staying here," said Dad.

"NO!" screamed Henry.

"YES!" screamed Dad.

I am sorry to say that Henry then had the longest, loudest, noisiest, shrillest, most horrible tantrum you can imagine.

Did you think that a horrid boy like Henry would like nothing better

than sleeping on
hard rocky ground
in a soggy sleeping
bag without a
pillow?

You thought
wrong.

Henry liked
comfy beds.

Henry liked crisp
sheets.

Henry liked hot
baths.

Henry liked
microwave dinners,
TV, and noise.

He did not like cold showers, fresh
air, and quiet.

Far off in the distance the sweet
sound of loud music drifted towards
them.

"Aren't you glad we're not staying in that awful noisy place?" said Dad.

"Oh yes," said Mum.

"Oh yes," said Perfect Peter.

Henry pretended he was a bulldozer come to knock down tents and squash campers.

"Henry, don't barge the tent!" yelled Dad.

Henry pretended he was a hungry *Tyrannosaurus Rex*.

"OW!" shrieked Peter.

"Henry, don't be horrid!" yelled Mum.

She looked up at the dark cloudy sky.

"It's going to rain," said Mum.

"Don't worry," said Dad. "It never rains when I'm camping."

"The boys and I will go and collect some more firewood," said Mum.

"I'm not moving," said Horrid Henry.

While Dad made a campfire, Henry played his boom-box as loud as he could, stomping in time to the terrible music of the Killer Boy Rats.

"Henry, turn that noise down this minute," said Dad.

Henry pretended not to hear.

"HENRY!" yelled Dad. "TURN THAT DOWN!"

Henry turned the volume down the teeniest tiniest fraction.

The terrible sounds of the Killer Boy Rats continued to boom over the quiet campsite.

Campers emerged from their tents and shook their fists. Dad switched off Henry's tape player.

"Anything wrong, Dad?" asked Henry, in his sweetest voice.

"No," said Dad.

Mum and Peter returned carrying armfuls of firewood.

It started to drizzle.

"This is fun," said Mum, slapping a mosquito.

"Isn't it?" said Dad. He was heating up some tins of baked beans.

The drizzle turned into a downpour.

The wind blew.

The campfire hissed, and went out.

"Never mind," said Dad brightly. "We'll eat our baked beans cold."

Mum was snoring.

Dad was snoring.

Peter was snoring.

Henry tossed and turned. But whichever way he turned in his damp sleeping bag, he seemed to be lying on sharp, pointy stones.

Above him, mosquitoes whined.

I'll never get to sleep, he thought, kicking Peter.

How am I going to bear this for fourteen days?

Around four o'clock on Day Five the family huddled inside the cold, damp, smelly tent listening to the howling wind and the pouring rain.

"Time for a walk!" said Dad.

"Great idea!" said Mum, sneezing. "I'll get the boots."

"Great idea!" said Peter, sneezing. "I'll get the macs."

"But it's pouring outside," said Henry.

"So?" said Dad. "What better time to go for a walk?"

"I'm not coming," said Horrid Henry.

"I am," said Perfect Peter. "I don't mind the rain."

Dad poked his head outside the tent.

"The rain has stopped," he said. "I'll remake the fire."

"I'm not coming," said Henry.

"We need more firewood," said Dad. "Henry can stay here and collect some. And make sure it's dry."

Henry poked his head outside the tent. The rain had stopped, but the sky was still cloudy. The fire spat.

I won't go, thought Henry. The forest will be all muddy and wet.

He looked round to see if there was any wood closer to home.

That was when he saw the thick, dry wooden pegs holding up all the tents.

Henry looked to the left.
Henry looked to the right.
No one was around.

If I just take a few pegs from each
tent, he thought, they'll never be
missed.

When Mum and Dad came back
they were delighted.

"What a lovely roaring fire," said
Mum.

"Clever you to find some dry
wood," said Dad.

The wind blew.

Henry dreamed he was floating in a cold river, floating, floating, floating.

He woke up. He shook his head. He *was* floating. The tent was filled with cold muddy water.

Then the tent collapsed on top of them.

Henry, Peter, Mum and Dad stood outside in the rain and stared at the river of water gushing through their collapsed tent.

All round them soaking wet campers were staring at their collapsed tents.

Peter sneezed.

Mum sneezed.

Dad sneezed.

Henry coughed, choked, spluttered and sneezed.

"I don't understand it," said Dad. "This tent *never* collapses."

"What are we going to do?" said Mum.

"I know," said Henry. "I've got a very good idea."

Two hours later Mum, Dad, Henry and Peter were sitting on a sofa-bed inside a tent as big as a house, eating crisps and watching TV.

The sun was shining. The sky was blue.

"Now this is what I call a holiday!" said Henry.

HORRID
HENRY
AND THE
SECRET CLUB

For Susan Winter, without whom . . .

CONTENTS

1

HORRID HENRY'S INJECTION

"AAGGHH!!"

"AAAGGGGHHH!!!!"

"AAAAAGGGGGHHHHH!!!!"

The horrible screams came from behind Nurse Needle's closed door.

Horrid Henry looked at his younger brother Perfect Peter. Perfect Peter looked at Horrid Henry. Then they both looked at their father, who stared straight ahead.

Henry and Peter were in Dr Dettol's waiting room.

Moody Margaret was there. So were Sour Susan, Anxious Andrew, Jolly Josh, Weepy William, Tough Toby, Lazy Linda, Clever Clare, Rude Ralph and just about everyone Henry knew. They were all waiting for the terrible moment when Nurse Needle would call their name.

Today was the worst day in the world. Today was – injection day.

Horrid Henry was not afraid of spiders.

He was not afraid of spooks.

He was not afraid of burglars, bad dreams, squeaky doors and things that go bump in the night. Only one thing scared him.

Just thinking about . . . about . . . Henry could barely even say the word – INJECTIONS – made him shiver and quiver and shake and quake.

Nurse Needle came into the waiting room.

Henry held his breath.

"Please let it be someone else," he prayed.

"William!" said Nurse Needle.

Weepy William burst into tears.

"Let's have none of that," said Nurse Needle. She took him firmly by the arm and closed the door behind him.

"I don't need an injection!" said Henry. "I feel fine."

"Injections stop you getting ill," said Dad. "Injections fight germs."

"I don't believe in germs," said Henry.

"I do," said Dad.

"I do," said Peter.

"Well, I don't," said Henry.

Dad sighed. "You're having an injection, and that's that."

"I don't mind injections," said Perfect Peter. "I know how good they are for me."

Horrid Henry pretended he was an alien who'd come from outer space to jab earthlings.

"OWW!" shrieked Peter.

"Don't be horrid, Henry!" shouted Dad.

"AAAAAAGGGGGHHHHHH!"

came the terrible screams from
behind Nurse Needle's door.
"AAAAAAGGGGGHHHHH!
NOOOOOOOO!"

Then Weepy William staggered
out, clutching his arm and wailing.

"Crybaby," said Henry.

"Just wait, Henry," sobbed
William.

Nurse Needle came into the
waiting room.

Henry closed his eyes.

"Don't pick me," he begged
silently. "Don't pick me."

"Susan!" said Nurse Needle.

Sour Susan crept into Nurse
Needle's office.

"AAAAAAGGGGGHHHHHH!"
came the terrible screams.
"AAAAAAGGGGGHHHHH!
NOOOOOOO!"

Then Sour Susan dragged herself
out, clutching her arm and snivelling.

"What a crybaby," said Henry.

"Well, we all know about *you*,
Henry," said Susan sourly.

"Oh yeah?" said Henry. "You
don't know anything."

Nurse Needle reappeared.

Henry hid his face behind his
hands.

I'll be so good if it's not me, he
thought. Please, let it be someone else.

"Margaret!" said Nurse Needle.

Henry relaxed.

"Hey, Margaret, did you know the needles are so big and sharp they can go right through your arm?" said Henry.

Moody Margaret ignored him and marched into Nurse Needle's office.

Henry could hardly wait for her terrible screams. Boy, would he tease that crybaby Margaret!

Silence.

Then Moody Margaret swaggered into the waiting room, proudly displaying a enormous plaster on her arm. She smiled at Henry.

"Ooh, Henry, you won't believe the needle she's using today," said Margaret. "It's as long as my leg."

"Shut up, Margaret," said Henry. He was breathing very fast and felt faint.

"Anything wrong, Henry?" asked Margaret sweetly.

"No," said Henry. He scowled at her. How dare she not scream and cry?

"Oh, good," said Margaret. "I just wanted to warn you because I've never seen such big fat whopping needles in all my life!"

Horrid Henry steadied himself. Today would be different.

He would be brave.

He would be fearless.

He would march into Nurse Needle's office, offer his arm, and dare her to do her worst. Yes, today was the day. Brave Henry, he would be called, the boy who laughed when the needle went in, the boy who asked for a second injection, the boy who –

"Henry!" said Nurse Needle.

"NO!" shrieked Henry. "Please, please, NO!"

"Yes," said Nurse Needle. "It's your turn now."

Henry forgot he was brave.

Henry forgot he was fearless.

Henry forgot everyone was watching him.

Henry started screaming and screeching and kicking.

"OW!" yelped Dad.

"OW!" yelped Perfect Peter.

"OW!" yelped Lazy Linda.

Then everyone started screaming and screeching.

"I don't want an injection!" shrieked Horrid Henry.

"I don't want an injection!" shrieked Anxious Andrew.

"I don't want an injection!" shrieked Tough Toby.

"Stop it," said Nurse Needle. "You need an injection and an injection is what you will get."

"Him first!" screamed Henry, pointing at Peter.

"You're such a baby, Henry," said Clever Clare.

That did it.

No one *ever* called Henry a baby and lived.

He kicked Clare as hard as he could. Clare screamed.

Nurse Needle and Dad each grabbed one of Henry's arms and dragged him howling into her office. Peter followed behind, whistling softly.

Henry wriggled free and dashed out. Dad nabbed him and brought him back. Nurse Needle's door clanged shut behind them.

Henry stood in the corner. He was trapped.

Nurse Needle kept her distance. Nurse Needle knew Henry. Last time he'd had an injection he'd kicked her.

Dr Dettol came in.

"What's the trouble, Nurse?" she asked.

"Him," said Nurse Needle. "He doesn't want an injection."

116

Dr Dettol kept her distance. Dr Dettol knew Henry. Last time he'd had an injection he'd bitten her.

"Take a seat, Henry," said Dr Dettol.

Henry collapsed in a chair. There was no escape.

"What a fuss over a little thing like an injection," said Dr Dettol. "Call me if you need me," she added, and left the room.

Henry sat on the chair, breathing hard. He tried not to look as Nurse Needle examined her gigantic pile of syringes.

But he could not stop himself peeking through his fingers. He watched as she got the injection ready, choosing the longest, sharpest, most wicked needle Henry had ever seen.

Then Nurse Needle approached, weapon in hand.

"Him first!" shrieked Henry.

Perfect Peter sat down and rolled up his sleeve.

"I'll go first," said Peter. "I don't mind."

"Oh," he said, as he was jabbed.

"That was perfect," said Nurse Needle.

"What a good boy you are," said Dad.

Perfect Peter smiled proudly.

Nurse Needle rearmed herself.

Horrid Henry shrank back in the chair. He looked around wildly.

Then Henry noticed the row of little medicine bottles lined up on the counter. Nurse Needle was filling her injections from them.

Henry looked closer. The labels

read: "Do NOT give injection if a child is feverish or seems ill."

Nurse Needle came closer, brandishing the injection. Henry coughed.

And closer. Henry sneezed.

And closer. Henry wheezed and rasped and panted.

Nurse Needle lowered her arm.

"Are you all right, Henry?"

"No," gasped Henry. "I'm ill. My chest hurts, my head hurts, my throat hurts."

Nurse Needle felt his sweaty forehead.

Henry coughed again, a dreadful throaty cough.

"I can't breathe," he choked. "Asthma."

"You don't have asthma, Henry," said Dad.

"I do, too," said Henry, gasping for breath.

Nurse Needle frowned.

"He is a little warm," she said.

"I'm ill," whispered Henry pathetically. "I feel terrible."

Nurse Needle put down her syringe.

"I think you'd better bring him back when he's feeling better," she said.

"All right," said Dad. He'd make sure Henry's mother brought him next time.

Henry wheezed and sneezed, moaned and groaned, all the way home. His parents put him straight to bed.

"Oh, Mum," said Henry, trying to sound as weak as possible. "Could you bring me some chocolate ice cream to soothe my throat? It really hurts."

"Of course,' said Mum. "You poor boy."

Henry snuggled down in the cool sheets. Ahh, this was the life.

"Oh, Mum," added Henry, coughing. "Could you bring up the

TV? Just in case my head stops hurting long enough for me to watch?"

"Of course," said Mum.

Boy, this was great! thought Henry.

No injection! No school tomorrow! Supper in bed!

There was a knock on the door. It must be Mum with his ice cream. Henry sat up in bed, then remembered he was ill. He lay back and closed his eyes.

"Come in, Mum," said Henry hoarsely.

"Hello Henry."

Henry opened his eyes. It wasn't Mum. It was Dr Dettol.

Henry closed his eyes and had a terrible coughing fit.

"What hurts?" said Dr Dettol.

"Everything," said Henry. "My head, my throat, my chest, my eyes, my ears, my back and my legs."

"Oh dear," said Dr Dettol.

She took out her stethoscope and listened to Henry's chest. All clear.

She stuck a little stick in his mouth and told him to say "AAAAAH." All clear.

She examined his eyes and ears, his back and his legs. Everything seemed fine.

"Well, Doctor?" said Mum.

Dr Dettol shook her head. She looked grave.

"He's very ill," said Dr Dettol. "There's only one cure."

"What?" said Mum.

"What?" said Dad.

"An injection!"

2

·····································

HORRID HENRY
AND THE
SECRET CLUB

"Halt! Who goes there?"

"Me."

"Who's me?" said Moody
Margaret.

"ME!" said Sour Susan.

"What's the password?"

"Uhhhh . . ." Sour Susan paused.
What was the password? She thought
and thought and thought.

"Potatoes?"

Margaret sighed loudly. Why was

she friends with such a stupid person?

"No it isn't."

"Yes it is," said Susan.

"Potatoes was last week's password," said Margaret.

"No it wasn't."

"Yes it was," said Moody Margaret. "It's my club and I decide."

There was a long pause.

"All right," said Susan sourly. "What *is* the password?"

"I don't know if I'm going to tell you," said Margaret. "I could be giving away a big secret to the enemy."

"But I'm not the enemy," said Susan. "I'm Susan."

"Shhhh!" said Margaret. "We don't want Henry to find out who's in the secret club."

Susan looked quickly over her shoulder. The enemy was nowhere to be seen. She whistled twice.

"All clear," said Sour Susan. "Now let me in."

Moody Margaret thought for a moment. Letting someone in without the password broke the first club rule.

"Prove to me you're Susan, and not the enemy pretending to be Susan," said Margaret.

"You know it's me," wailed Susan.

"Prove it."

Susan stuck her foot into the tent.

"I'm wearing the black patent leather shoes with the blue flowers I always wear."

"No good," said Margaret. "The enemy could have stolen them."

"I'm speaking with Susan's voice and I look like Susan," said Susan.

"No good," said Margaret. "The enemy could be a master of disguise."

Susan stamped her foot. "And I know that you were the one who pinched Helen and I'm going to tell Miss . . ."

"Come closer to the tent flap," said Margaret.

Susan bent over.

"Now listen to me," said Margaret. "Because I'm only going to tell you once. When a secret club member wants to come in they say 'NUNGA.' Anyone inside answers back, 'Nunga Nu.' That's how I know it's you and you know it's me."

"Nunga," said Sour Susan.

"Nunga Nu," said Moody Margaret. "Enter."

Susan entered the club. She gave

the secret handshake, sat down on her box and sulked.

"You knew it was me all along," said Susan.

Margaret scowled at her.

"That's not the point. If you don't want to obey the club rules you can leave."

Susan didn't move.

"Can I have a biscuit?" she said.

Margaret smiled graciously. "Have two," she said. "Then we'll get down to business."

Meanwhile, hidden under a bush behind some strategically placed branches, another top secret meeting was taking place in the next door garden.

"I think that's everything," said the Leader. "I shall now put the plans into action."

"What am I going to do?" said Perfect Peter.

"Stand guard," said Horrid Henry.

"I always have to stand guard," said Peter, as the Leader crept out.

"It's not fair."

★

"Have you brought your spy report?" asked Margaret.

"Yes," said Susan.

"Read it aloud," said Margaret.

Susan took out a piece of paper and read:

"I watched the enemy's house for two hours yesterday morning –"

"Which morning?" interrupted Margaret.

"Saturday morning," said Susan. "A lady with grey hair and a beret walked past."

"What colour was the beret?" said Margaret.

"I don't know," said Susan.

"Call yourself a spy and you don't know what colour the beret was," said Margaret.

"Can I please continue with my report?" said Susan.

"I'm not stopping you," said
Margaret.

"Then I saw the enemy leave the
house with his brother and mother.
The enemy kicked his brother twice.
His mother shouted at him. Then I
saw the postman —"

"NUNGA!" screeched a voice
from outside.

Margaret and Susan froze.

"NUNGA!!!"

screeched the voice again. "I know you're in there!"

"Aaaahh!" squeaked Susan. "It's Henry!"

"Quick! Hide!" hissed Margaret.

The secret spies crouched behind two boxes.

"You told him our password!" hissed Margaret. "How dare you!"

"Wasn't me!" hissed Susan. "I couldn't even remember it, so how could I have told him? You told him!"

"Didn't," hissed Margaret.

"NUNGA!!!" screeched Henry again. "You have to let me in! I know the password."

"What do we do?" hissed Susan. "You said anyone who knows the password enters."

"For the last time,

NUNGAAAAA!" shouted Horrid
Henry.

"Nunga Nu," said Margaret.
"Enter."

Henry swaggered into the tent.
Margaret glared at him.

"Don't mind if I do," said Henry,
grabbing all the chocolate biscuits and
stuffing them into his mouth. Then
he sprawled on the rug, scattering
crumbs everywhere.

"What are you doing?" said Horrid
Henry.

"Nothing," said Moody Margaret.

"Nothing," said Sour Susan.

"You are, too," said Henry.

"Mind your own business," said
Margaret. "Now, Susan, let's vote on
whether to allow boys in. I vote
No."

"I vote No, too," said Susan.

"Sorry, Henry, you can't join. Now leave."

"No," said Henry.

"LEAVE," said Margaret.

"Make me," said Henry.

Margaret took a deep breath. Then she opened her mouth and screamed. No one could scream as loud, or as long, or as piercingly, as Moody Margaret. After a few moments, Susan started screaming too.

Henry got to his feet, knocking over the crate they used as a table.

"Watch out," said Henry. "Because the Purple Hand will be back!" He turned to go.

Moody Margaret sprang up behind him and pushed him through the flap. Henry landed in a heap outside.

"Can't get me!" shouted Henry. He picked himself up and jumped over the wall. "The Purple Hand is the best!"

"Oh yeah," muttered Margaret. "We'll see about that."

Henry checked over his shoulder to make sure no one was watching. Then he crept back to his fort.

"Smelly toads," he whispered to the guard.

The branches parted. Henry

climbed in.

"Did you attack them?" said Peter.

"Of course," said Henry. "Didn't you hear Margaret screaming?"

"I was the one who heard their password, so I think I should have gone," said Peter.

"Whose club is this?" said Henry.

The corners of Peter's mouth began to turn down.

"Right, out!" said Henry.

"Sorry!" said Peter. "Please, Henry, can I be a real member of the Purple Hand?"

"No," said Henry. "You're too young. And don't you dare come into the fort when I'm not here."

"I won't," said Peter.

"Good," said Henry. "Now here's the plan. I'm going to set a booby trap in Margaret's tent. Then when

HORRID HENRY AND THE SECRET CLUB

she goes in . . ." Henry shrieked with
laughter as he pictured Moody
Margaret covered in cold muddy
water.

All was not well back at Moody
Margaret's Secret Club.
"It's your fault," said Margaret.
"It isn't," said Susan.
"You're such a blabbermouth, and
you're a terrible spy."
"I am not," said Susan.
"Well, I'm Leader, and I ban you
from the club for a week for breaking
our sacred rule and telling the enemy
our password. Now go away."
"Oh please let me stay," said
Susan.
"No," said Margaret.
Susan knew there was no point
arguing with Margaret when she got

that horrible bossy look on her face.

"You're so mean," said Susan.

Moody Margaret picked up a book and started to read.

Sour Susan got up and left.

"I know what I'll do to fix Henry," thought Margaret. "I'll set a booby trap in Henry's fort. Then when he goes in . . ." Margaret shrieked with laughter as she pictured Horrid Henry covered in cold muddy water.

Just before lunch Henry sneaked into Margaret's garden holding a plastic bucket of water and some string. He stretched the string just above the ground across the entrance and suspended the bucket above, with the other end of the string tied round it.

Just after lunch Margaret sneaked into Henry's garden holding a bucket of water and some string. She stretched the string across the fort's entrance and rigged up the bucket. What she wouldn't give to see Henry soaking wet when he tripped over the string and pulled the bucket of water down on him.

Perfect Peter came into the garden carrying a ball. Henry wouldn't play with him and there was nothing to do.

Why shouldn't I go into the fort? thought Peter. I helped build it.

Next door, Sour Susan slipped into the garden. She was feeling sulky.

Why shouldn't I go into the tent? thought Susan. It's my club too.

Perfect Peter walked into the fort and tripped.

CRASH! SPLASH!

Sour Susan walked into the tent and tripped.

CRASH! SPLASH!

Horrid Henry heard howls. He ran into the garden whooping.

"Ha! Ha! Margaret! Gotcha!"

Then he stopped.

Moody Margaret heard screams. She ran into the garden cheering.

"Ha! Ha! Henry! Gotcha!"

Then she stopped.

"That's it!" shrieked Peter. "I'm leaving!"

"But it wasn't me," said Henry.

"That's it!" sobbed Susan. "I quit!"

"But it wasn't me," said Margaret.

"Rats!" said Henry.

"Rats!" said Margaret.

They glared at each other.

3

PERFECT PETER'S HORRID DAY

"Henry, use your fork!" said Dad.

"*I'm* using my fork," said Peter.

"Henry, sit down!" said Mum.

"*I'm* sitting down," said Peter.

"Henry, stop spitting!" said Dad.

"*I'm* not spitting," said Peter.

"Henry, chew with your mouth shut!" said Mum.

"*I'm* chewing with my mouth shut," said Peter.

"Henry, don't make a mess!" said Dad.

"*I'm* not making a mess," said Peter.

"What?" said Mum.

Perfect Peter was not having a perfect day.

Mum and Dad are too busy yelling at Henry all the time to notice how good *I* am, thought Peter.

When was the last time Mum and Dad had said, "Marvellous, Peter, you're using your fork!" "Wonderful, Peter, you're sitting down!" "Superb, Peter, you're not spitting!" "Fabulous, Peter, you're chewing with your mouth shut!" "Perfect, Peter, you never make a mess!"

Perfect Peter dragged himself upstairs.

Everyone just expects me to be perfect, thought Peter, as he wrote his Aunt Agnes a thank you note for the super thermal vests. It's not fair.

From downstairs came the sound

of raised voices.

"Henry, get your muddy shoes off the sofa!" yelled Dad.

"Henry, stop being so horrid!" yelled Mum.

Then Perfect Peter started to think.

What if *I* were horrid? thought Peter.

Peter's mouth dropped open. What a horrid thought! He looked around quickly, to see if anyone had noticed.

He was alone in his immaculate bedroom. No one would ever know he'd thought such a terrible thing.

But imagine being horrid. No, that would never do.

Peter finished his letter, read a few pages of his favourite magazine *Best Boy*, got into bed and turned off his light without being asked.

Imagine being horrid.

What *if* I were horrid, thought Peter. I wonder what would happen?

When Peter woke up the next morning, he did not dash downstairs to get breakfast ready. Instead, he lazed in bed for an extra five minutes.

When he finally got out of bed Peter did not straighten the duvet.

Nor did Peter plump his pillows.

Instead Peter looked at his tidy bedroom and had a very wicked thought.

Quickly, before he could change his mind, he took off his pyjama top and did not fold it neatly. Instead he dropped it on the floor.

Mum came in.

"Good morning, darling. You must be tired, sleeping in."

Peter hoped Mum would notice his

untidy room.

But Mum did not say anything.

"Notice anything, Mum?" said
Peter.

Mum looked around.

"No," said Mum.

"Oh," said Peter.

"What?" said Mum.

"I haven't made my bed," said
Peter.

"Clever you to remember it's
washday," said Mum. She stripped
the sheets and duvet cover, then

swooped and picked up Peter's
pyjama top.

"Thank you, dear," said Mum. She
smiled and left.

Peter frowned. Clearly, he would
need to work harder at being horrid.

He looked at his beautifully
arranged books.

"No!" he gasped, as a dreadful
thought sneaked into his head.

Then Peter squared his shoulders.
Today was his horrid day, and horrid
he would be. He went up to his
books and knocked them over.

"HENRY!" bellowed Dad. "Get
up this minute!"

Henry slumped past Peter's door.

Peter decided he would call Henry
a horrid name.

"Hello, Ugly," said Peter. Then he
went wild and stuck out his tongue.

Henry marched into Peter's bedroom. He glared at Peter.

"What did you call me?" said Henry.

Peter screamed.

Mum ran into the room.

"Stop being horrid, Henry! Look what a mess you've made in here!"

"He called me Ugly," said Henry.

"Of course he didn't," said Mum.

"He did too," said Henry.

"Peter never calls people names," said Mum. "Now pick up those books you knocked over."

"I didn't knock them over," said Henry.

"Well, who did, then, the man in the moon?" said Mum.

Henry pointed at Peter.

"He did," said Henry.

"*Did* you, Peter?" asked Mum.

Peter wanted to be really really horrid and tell a lie. But he couldn't.

"I did it, Mum," said Peter. Boy, would he get told off now.

"Don't be silly, of course you didn't," said Mum. "You're just saying that to protect Henry."

Mum smiled at Peter and frowned at Henry.

"Now leave Peter alone and get dressed," said Mum.

"But it's the weekend," said Henry.

"So?" said Mum.

"But Peter's not dressed."

"I'm sure he was just about to get dressed before your barged in," said Mum. "See? He's already taken his pyjama top off."

"I don't want to get dressed," said Peter boldly.

"You poor boy," said Mum. "You must be feeling ill. Pop back into bed and I'll bring your breakfast up. Just let me put some clean sheets on."

Perfect Peter scowled a tiny scowl. Clearly, he wasn't very good at being horrid yet. He would have to try harder.

At lunch Peter ate pasta with his
fingers. No one noticed.

Then Henry scooped up pasta with
both fists and slurped some into his
mouth.

"Henry! Use your fork!" said Dad.

Peter spat into his plate.

"Peter, are you choking?" said
Dad.

Henry spat across the table.

"Henry! Stop that disgusting
spitting this instant!" said Mum.

Peter chewed with his mouth open.

"Peter, is there something wrong
with your teeth?" asked Mum.

Henry chomped and dribbled and
gulped with his mouth as wide open
as possible.

"Henry! This is your last warning.
Keep your mouth shut when you
eat!" shouted Dad.

Peter did not understand. Why didn't anyone notice how horrid he was? He stretched out his foot and kicked Henry under the table.

Henry kicked him back harder.

Peter shrieked.

Henry got told off. Peter got dessert.

Perfect Peter did not know what to do. No matter how hard he tried to be horrid, nothing seemed to work.

"Now boys," said Mum, "Grandma is coming for tea this afternoon. Please keep the house tidy and leave the chocolates alone."

"What chocolates?" said Henry.

"Never you mind," said Mum. "You'll have some when Grandma gets here."

Then Peter had a truly stupendously horrid idea. He left the

table without waiting to be excused
and sneaked into the sitting room.

Peter searched high. Peter searched
low. Then Peter found a large box of
chocolates hidden behind some
books.

Peter opened the box. Then he
took a tiny bite out of every single
chocolate. When he found good ones
with gooey chocolate fudge centres
he ate them. The yucky raspberry and
strawberry and lemon creams he put
back.

Hee Hee, thought Peter. He felt excited. What he had done was absolutely awful. Mum and Dad were sure to notice.

Then Peter looked round the tidy sitting room. Why not mess it up a bit?

Peter grabbed a cushion from the sofa. He was just about to fling it on the floor when he heard someone sneaking into the room.

"What are you doing?" said Henry.

"Nothing, Ugly," said Peter.

"Don't call me Ugly, Toad," said Henry.

"Don't call me Toad, Ugly," said Peter.

"Toad!"

"Ugly!"

"TOAD!"

"UGLY!"

Mum and Dad ran in.

"Henry!" shouted Dad. "Stop being horrid!"

"I'm not being horrid!" said Henry. "Peter is calling me names."

Mum and Dad looked at each other. What was going on?

"Don't lie, Henry," said Mum.

"I did call him a name, Mum," said Peter. "I called him Ugly because he is ugly. So there."

Mum stared at Peter.

Dad stared at Peter.

Henry stared at Peter.

"If Peter did call you a name, it's because you called him one first," said Mum. "Now leave Peter alone."

Mum and Dad left.

"Serves you right, Henry," said Peter.

"You're very strange today," said Henry.

"No I'm not," said Peter.

"Oh yes you are," said Henry. "You can't fool me. Listen, want to play a trick on Grandma?"

"No!" said Peter.

Ding dong.

"Grandma's here!" called Dad.

Mum, Dad, Henry, Peter and Grandma sat down together in the sitting room.

"Let me take your bag, Grandma," said Henry sweetly.

"Thank you dear," said Grandma.

When no one was looking Henry took Grandma's glasses out of her bag and hid them behind Peter's cushion.

Mum and Dad passed around tea and home-made biscuits on the best china plates.

Peter sat on the edge of the sofa and held his breath. Any second now Mum would get out the box of half-eaten chocolates.

Mum stood up and got the box.

"Peter, would you like to pass round the chocolates?" said Mum.

"Okay," said Peter. His knees felt wobbly. Everyone was about to find out what a horrid thing he had done.

Peter held out the box.

"Would you like a chocolate, Mum?" said Peter. His heart pounded.

"No thanks," said Mum.

"What about me?" said Henry.

"Would you like a chocolate, Dad?" said Peter. His hands shook.

"No thanks," said Dad.

"What about me!" said Henry.

"Shh, Henry," said Mum. "Don't be so rude."

"Would you like a chocolate, Grandma?" said Peter.

There was no escape now. Grandma loved chocolates.

"Yes, please!" said Grandma. She peered closely into the box. "Let me see, what shall I choose? Now, where are my specs?"

Grandma reached into her bag and fumbled about.

"That's funny," said Grandma. "I was sure I'd brought them. Never mind."

Grandma reached into the box, chose a chocolate and popped it into her mouth.

"Oh," said Grandma. "Strawberry cream. Go on, Peter, have a chocolate."

"No thanks," said Peter.

"WHAT ABOUT ME!" screamed Horrid Henry.

"None for you," said Dad. "That's not how you ask."

Peter gritted his teeth. If no one was going to notice the chewed chocolates he'd have to do it himself.

"I will have a chocolate," announced Peter loudly. "Hey! Who's eaten all the fudge ones? And who's taken bites out of the rest?"

"Henry!" yelled Mum. "I've told you a million times to leave the chocolates alone!"

"It wasn't me!" said Henry. "It was Peter!"

"Stop blaming Peter," said Dad. "You know he never eats sweets."

"It's not fair!" shrieked Henry. Then he snatched the box from Peter. "I want some CHOCOLATES!"

Peter snatched it back. The open box fell to the floor. Chocolates flew everywhere.

"HENRY, GO TO YOUR ROOM!" yelled Mum.

"IT'S NOT FAIR!" screeched Henry. "I'll get you for this, Peter!"

Then Horrid Henry ran out of the room, slamming the door behind him.

Grandma patted the sofa beside her. Peter sat down. He could not believe it. What did a boy have to do to get noticed?

"How's my best boy?" asked Grandma.

Peter sighed.

Grandma gave him a big hug. "You're the best boy in the world, Peter, did you know that?"

Peter glowed. Grandma was right! He was the best.

But wait. Today he was horrid.

NO! He was perfect. His horrid

day was over.

He was much happier being perfect, anyway. Being horrid was horrible.

I've had my horrid day, thought Peter. Now I can be perfect again.

What a marvellous idea. Peter smiled and leaned back against the cushion.

CRUNCH!

"Oh dear," said Grandma. "That sounds like my specs. I wonder how they got there."

Mum looked at Peter.

Dad looked at Peter.

"It wasn't me!" said Peter.

"Of course not," said Grandma. "I must have dropped them. Silly me."

"Hmmmn," said Dad.

Perfect Peter ran into the kitchen and looked about. Now that I'm perfect again, what good deeds can I do? he thought.

Then Peter noticed all the dirty tea cups and plates piled up on the worktop. He had never done the washing up all by himself before. Mum and Dad would be so pleased.

Peter carefully washed and dried all the dishes.

Then he stacked them up and carried them to the cupboard.

"BOOOOOOO!" shrieked Horrid Henry, leaping out from behind the door.

CRASH!

Henry vanished.

Mum and Dad ran in.

The best china lay in pieces all over the floor.

"PETER!!!" yelled Mum and Dad.

"YOU HORRID BOY!" yelled Mum.

"GO TO YOUR ROOM!" yelled Dad.

"But . . . but . . ." gasped Peter.

"NO BUTS!" shouted Mum. "GO! Oh, my lovely dishes!"

Perfect Peter ran to his room.

"AHHHHHHHHHHHH!" shrieked Peter.

4

HORRID HENRY'S BIRTHDAY PARTY

February was Horrid Henry's favourite month.

His birthday was in February.

"It's my birthday soon!" said Henry every day after Christmas. "And my birthday party! Hurray!"

February was Horrid Henry's parents' least favourite month.

"It's Henry's birthday soon," said Dad, groaning.

"And his birthday party," said Mum, groaning even louder.

Every year they thought Henry's

169

birthday parties could not get worse.
But they always did.

Every year Henry's parents said
they would never ever let Henry have
a birthday party again. But every year
they gave Henry one absolutely last
final chance.

Henry had big plans for this year's
party.

"I want to go to Lazer Zap," said
Henry. He'd been to Lazer Zap for
Tough Toby's party. They'd had a
great time dressing up as spacemen
and blasting each other in dark
tunnels all afternoon.

"NO!" said Mum. "Too violent."

"I agree," said Dad.

"And too expensive," said Mum.

"I agree," said Dad.

There was a moment's silence.

"However," said Dad, "it does

mean the party wouldn't be here."

Mum looked at Dad. Dad looked at Mum.

"How do I book?" said Mum.

"Hurray!" shrieked Henry. "Zap! Zap! Zap!"

Horrid Henry sat in his fort holding a pad of paper. On the front cover in big capital letters Henry wrote:

HENRY'S PARTY PLANS.
TOP SECRET!!!!

At the top of the first page Henry had written:

GUESTS

A long list followed. Then Henry stared at the names and chewed his pencil.

Actually, I don't want Margaret, thought Henry. Too moody.

He crossed out Moody Margaret's

name.

And I definitely don't want Susan. Too crabby.

In fact, I don't want any girls at all, thought Henry. He crossed out Clever Clare and Lazy Linda.

Then there was Anxious Andrew.

Nope, thought Henry, crossing him off. He's no fun.

Toby was possible, but Henry didn't really like him.

Out went Tough Toby.

William?

No way, thought Henry. He'll be crying the second he gets zapped.

Out went Weepy William.

Ralph?

Henry considered. Ralph would be good because he was sure to get into trouble. On the other hand, he hadn't invited Henry to *his* party.

Rude Ralph was struck off.

So were Babbling Bob, Jolly Josh, Greedy Graham and Dizzy Dave. And absolutely no way was Peter coming anywhere near him on his birthday.

Ahh, that was better. No horrid kids would be coming to *his* party.

There was only one problem. Every single name was crossed off.

No guests meant no presents.

Henry looked at his list. Margaret was a moody old grouch and he hated her, but she did sometimes give good gifts. He still had the jumbo box of day-glo slime she'd given him last year.

And Toby *had* invited Henry to *his* party.

And Dave was always spinning round like a top, falling and knocking

things over which was fun. Graham
would eat too much and burp. And
Ralph was sure to say rude words and
make all the grown-ups angry.

Oh, let them all come, thought
Henry. Except Peter, of course. The
more guests I have, the more presents
I get!

Henry turned to the next page and wrote:

PRESENTS I WANT
Super Soaker 2000, the best water
blaster ever
Spy Fax
Micro Machines
Slime
GameBoy
Inter-galactic Samurai Gorillas
Stink bombs
Pet rats
Whoopee cushion
25-gear mountain bike
Money

He'd leave the list lying around where Mum and Dad were sure to find it.

"I've done the menu for the party,"

said Mum. "What do you think?"

MUM'S MENU
carrot sticks
cucumber sandwiches
peanut butter sandwiches
grapes
raisins
apple juice
carrot cake

"Blecccccch," said Henry. "I don't want that horrible food at my party. I want food that I like."

HENRY'S MENU
Pickled Onion Monster Munch
Smoky Spider Shreddies
Super Spicy Hedgehog Crisps
Crunchy Crackles
Twizzle Fizzle Sticks
Purple Planet-buster Drink

chocolate bars
chocolate eggs
Chocolate Monster Cake

"You can't just have junk food," said Mum.

"It's not junk food," said Henry. "Crisps are made from potatoes, and Monster Munch has onions – that's two vegetables."

"Henry . . ." said Mum. She looked fierce.

Henry looked at his menu. Then he added, in small letters at the bottom:

peanut butter sandwiches

"But only in the middle of the table," said Henry. "So no one has to eat them who doesn't want them."

"All right," said Mum. Years of

fighting with Henry about his parties had worn her down.

"And Peter's not coming," said Henry.

"What?!" said Perfect Peter, looking up from polishing his shoes.

"Peter is your brother. Of course he's invited."

Henry scowled.

"But he'll ruin everything."

"No Peter, no party," said Mum.

Henry pretended he was a fire-breathing dragon.

"Owww!" shrieked Peter.

"Don't be horrid, Henry!" yelled Mum.

"All right," said Henry. "He can come. But you'd better keep out of my way," he hissed at Peter.

"Mum!" wailed Peter. "Henry's being mean to me."

"Stop it, Henry," said Mum.

Henry decided to change the subject fast.

"What about party bags?" said Henry. "I want everyone to have Slime, and loads and loads and loads of sweets! Dirt Balls, Nose Pickers and Foam Teeth are the best."

"We'll see," said Mum. She looked at the calendar. Only two more days. Soon it would be over.

Henry's birthday arrived at last.

"Happy birthday, Henry!" said Mum.

"Happy birthday, Henry!" said Dad.

"Happy birthday, Henry!" said Peter.

"Where are my presents?" said Henry.

Dad pointed. Horrid Henry attacked the pile.

Mum and Dad had given him a *First Encyclopedia*, Scrabble, a fountain pen, a hand-knitted cardigan, a globe, and three sets of vests and pants.

"Oh," said Henry. He pushed the dreadful presents aside.

"Anything else?" he asked hopefully. Maybe they were keeping the super soaker for last.

"I've got a present for you," said Peter. "I chose it myself."

Henry tore off the wrapping paper. It was a tapestry kit.

"Yuck!" said Henry.

"I'll have it if you don't want it," said Peter.

"No!" said Henry, snatching up the kit.

"Wasn't it a great idea to have Henry's party at Lazer Zap?" said Dad.

182

"Yes," said Mum. "No mess, no fuss."

They smiled at each other.

Ring ring.

Dad answered the phone. It was the Lazer Zap lady.

"Hello! I was just ringing to check the birthday boy's name," she said. "We like to announce it over our loudspeaker during the party."

Dad gave Henry's name.

A terrible scream came from the other end of the phone. Dad held the receiver away from his ear.

The shrieking and screaming continued.

"Hmmmn," said Dad. "I see. Thank you."

Dad hung up. He looked pale.

"Henry!"

"Yeah?"

"Is it true that you wrecked the place when you went to Lazer Zap with Toby?" said Dad.

"No!" said Henry. He tried to look harmless.

"And trampled on several children?"

"No!" said Henry.

"Yes you did," said Perfect Peter. "And what about all the lasers you broke?"

"What lasers?" said Henry.

"And the slime you put in the space suits?" said Peter.

"That wasn't me, telltale," shrieked Henry. "What about my party?"

"I'm afraid Lazer Zap have banned you," said Dad.

"But what about Henry's party?" said Mum. She looked pale.

184

"But what about my party?!"
wailed Henry. "I want to go to Lazer
Zap!"

"Never mind," said Dad brightly.
"I know lots of good games."

Ding dong.

It was the first guest, Sour Susan.
She held a large present.

Henry snatched the package.

It was a pad of paper and some felt
tip pens.

"How lovely," said Mum. "What do you say, Henry?"

"I've already got that," said Henry.

"Henry!" said Mum. "Don't be horrid!"

I don't care, thought Henry. This was the worst day of his life.

Ding dong.

It was the second guest, Anxious Andrew. He held a tiny present.

Henry snatched the package.

"It's awfully small," said Henry, tearing off the wrapping. "And it smells."

It was a box of animal soaps.

"How super," said Dad. "What do you say, Henry?"

"Ugghhh!" said Henry.

"Henry!" said Dad. "Don't be horrid."

Henry stuck out his lower lip.

"It's my party and I'll do what I want," muttered Henry.

"Watch your step, young man," said Dad.

Henry stuck out his tongue behind Dad's back.

More guests arrived.

Lazy Linda gave him a "Read and Listen Cassette of favourite fairy tales: Cinderella, Snow White, and Sleeping Beauty."

"Fabulous," said Mum.

"Yuck!" said Henry.

Clever Clare handed him a square package.

Henry held it by the corners.

"It's a book," he groaned.

"My favourite present!" said Peter.

"Wonderful," said Mum. "What is it?"

Henry unwrapped it slowly.

"*Cook Your Own Healthy Nutritious Food.*"

"Great!" said Perfect Peter. "Can I borrow it?"

"NO!" screamed Henry. Then he threw the book on the floor and stomped on it.

"Henry!" hissed Mum. "I'm warning you. When someone gives you a present you say thank you."

Rude Ralph was the last to arrive.

He handed Henry a long rectangular package wrapped in newspaper.

It was a Super Soaker 2000 water blaster.

"Oh," said Mum.

"Put it away," said Dad.

"Thank you Ralph," beamed Henry. "Just what I wanted."

"Let's start with Pass the Parcel," said Dad.

"I hate Pass the Parcel," said Horrid Henry. What a horrible party this was.

"I love Pass the Parcel," said Perfect Peter.

"I don't want to play," said Sour Susan.

"When do we eat?" said Greedy Graham.

Dad started the music.

"Pass the parcel, William," said Dad.

"No!" shrieked William. "It's mine!"

"But the music is still playing," said Dad.

William burst into tears.

Horrid Henry tried to snatch the parcel.

Dad stopped the music.

William stopped crying instantly and tore off the wrapping.

"A granola bar," he said.

"That's a terrible prize," said Rude Ralph.

"Is it my turn yet?" said Anxious Andrew.

"When do we eat?" said Greedy Graham.

"I hate Pass the Parcel," screamed

Henry. "I want to play something
else."

"Musical Statues!" announced
Mum brightly.

"You're out, Henry," said Dad.
"You moved."

"I didn't," said Henry.

"Yes you did," said Toby.

"No I didn't," said Henry. "I'm
not leaving."

"That's not fair," shrieked Sour
Susan.

"I'm not playing," whined Dizzy
Dave.

"I'm tired," sulked Lazy Linda.

"I hate Musical Statues," moaned
Moody Margaret.

"Where's my prize?" demanded
Rude Ralph.

"A book mark?" said Ralph.

"That's it?"

"Tea time!" said Dad.

The children pushed and shoved their way to the table, grabbing and snatching at the food.

"I hate fizzy drinks," said Tough Toby.

"I feel sick," said Greedy Graham.

"Where are the carrot sticks?" said Perfect Peter.

Horrid Henry sat at the head of the table.

He didn't feel like throwing food at Clare.

He didn't feel like rampaging with Toby and Ralph.

He didn't even feel like kicking Peter.

He wanted to be at Lazer Zap.

Then Henry had a wonderful,

spectacular idea. He got up and
sneaked out of the room.

"Party bags," said Dad.

"What's in them?" said Tough
Toby.

"Seedlings," said Mum.

"Where are the sweets?" said
Greedy Graham.

"This is the worst party bag I've
ever had," said Rude Ralph.

There was a noise outside.

Then Henry burst into the kitchen,
supersoaker in hand.

"ZAP! ZAP! ZAP!" shrieked Henry, drenching everyone with water. "Ha! Ha! Gotcha!"

Splat went the cake.

Splash went the drinks.

"EEEEEEEEEEEEEKKK!" shrieked the sopping wet children.

"HENRY!!!!!" yelled Mum and Dad.

"YOU HORRID BOY!" yelled Mum. Water dripped from her hair. "GO TO YOUR ROOM!"

"THIS IS YOUR LAST PARTY EVER!" yelled Dad. Water dripped from his clothes.

But Henry didn't care. They said that every year.

HORRID HENRY

TRICKS THE TOOTH FAIRY

For Victor and Susan Bers,
and all our good times

CONTENTS

1

HORRID HENRY TRICKS THE TOOTH FAIRY

"It's not fair!" shrieked Horrid Henry. He trampled on Dad's new flower-bed, squashing the pansies. "It's just not fair!"

Moody Margaret had lost two teeth. Sour Susan had lost three. Clever Clare lost two in one day. Rude Ralph had lost four, two top and two bottom, and could spit to the blackboard from his desk. Greedy Graham's teeth were pouring out. Even Weepy William had lost one – and that was ages ago.

Every day someone swaggered into school showing off a big black toothy gap and waving fifty pence or even a pound that the Tooth Fairy had brought. Everyone, that is, but Henry.

"It's not fair!" shouted Henry again. He yanked on his teeth. He pulled, he pushed, he tweaked, and he tugged.

They would not budge.

His teeth were superglued to his gums.

"Why me?" moaned Henry, stomping on the petunias. "Why am I the only one who hasn't lost a tooth?"

Horrid Henry sat in his fort and scowled. He was sick and tired of other kids flaunting their ugly wobbly teeth and disgusting holes in their gums. The next person who so much as mentioned the word "tooth" had better watch out.

"HENRY!" shouted a squeaky little voice. "Where are you?"

Horrid Henry hid behind the branches.

"I know you're in the fort, Henry," said Perfect Peter.

"Go away!" said Henry.

"Look, Henry," said Peter. "I've got something wonderful to show you."

Henry scowled. "What?"

"You have to see it," said Peter.

Peter never had anything good to show. His idea of something wonderful was a new stamp, or a book about plants, or a gold star from his teacher saying how perfect he'd been. Still . . .

Henry crawled out.

"This had better be good," he said. "Or you're in big trouble."

Peter held out his fist and opened it.

There was something small and white in Peter's hand. It looked like . . . no, it couldn't be.

Henry stared at Peter. Peter smiled as

wide as he could. Henry's jaw dropped.
This was impossible. His eyes must be
playing tricks on him.

Henry blinked. Then he blinked again.

His eyes were not playing tricks.
Perfect Peter, his *younger* brother, had a
black gap at the bottom of his mouth
where a tooth had been.

Henry grabbed Peter. "You've
coloured in your tooth with black crayon,
you faker."

"Have not!" shrieked Peter. "It fell
out. See."

Peter proudly poked his finger through
the hole in his mouth.

It was true. Perfect Peter had lost a
tooth. Henry felt as if a fist had slammed
into his stomach.

"Told you," said Peter. He smiled
again at Henry.

Henry could not bear to look at Peter's
gappy teeth a second longer. This was the
worst thing that had ever happened to
him.

"I hate you!" shrieked Henry. He was
a volcano pouring hot molten lava on to
the puny human foolish enough to get in
his way.

"AAAAGGGGHHHH!" screeched
Peter, dropping the tooth.

Henry grabbed it.

"OWWWW!" yelped Peter. "Give
me back my tooth!"

"Stop being horrid, Henry!" shouted
Mum.

Henry dangled the tooth in front of
Peter.

"Nah nah ne nah nah," jeered Henry.

Peter burst into tears.

"Give me back my tooth!" screamed
Peter.

Mum ran into the garden.

"Give Peter his tooth this minute,"
said Mum.

"No," said Henry.

Mum looked fierce. She put out her
hand. "Give it to me right now."

Henry dropped the tooth on the
ground.

"There," said Horrid Henry.

"That's it, Henry," said Mum. "No pudding tonight."

Henry was too miserable to care.

Peter scooped up his tooth. "Look, Mum," said Peter.

"My big boy!" said Mum, giving him a hug. "How wonderful."

"I'm going to use my money from the Tooth Fairy to buy some stamps for my collection," said Peter.

"What a good idea," said Mum.

Henry stuck out his tongue.

"Henry's sticking out his tongue at me," said Peter.

"Stop it, Henry," said Mum. "Peter, keep that tooth safe for the Tooth Fairy."

"I will," said Peter. He closed his fist tightly round the tooth.

205

Henry sat in his fort. If a tooth wouldn't fall out, he would have to help it. But what to do? He could take a hammer and smash one out. Or he could tie string round a tooth, tie the string round a door handle and slam the door. Eek! Henry grabbed his jaw.

On second thoughts, perhaps not. Maybe there was a less painful way of losing a tooth. What was it the dentist always said? Eat too many sweets and your teeth will fall out?

Horrid Henry sneaked into the kitchen. He looked to the right. He looked to the left. No one was there. From the sitting room came the screechy scratchy sound of Peter practising his cello.

Henry dashed to the cupboard where Mum kept the sweet jar. Sweet day was Saturday, and today was Thursday. Two whole days before he got into trouble.

Henry stuffed as many sticky sweets into his mouth as fast as he could.

Chomp Chomp Chomp Chomp.

Chomp Chew Chomp Chew.

Chompa Chew Chompa Chew.

Chompa . . . Chompa . . .

Chompa . . .

Chompa . . .

Chew.

Henry's jaw started to slow down. He put the last sticky toffee in his mouth and forced his teeth to move up and down.

Henry started to feel sick. His teeth felt even sicker. He wiggled them hopefully. After all that sugar one was sure to fall out. He could see all the comics he would buy with his pound already.

Henry wiggled his teeth again. And again.

Nothing moved.

Rats, thought Henry. His mouth hurt. His gums hurt. His tummy hurt. What did a boy have to do to get a tooth?

Then Henry had a wonderful, spectacular idea. It was so wonderful that he hugged himself. Why should Peter get a pound from the Tooth Fairy? Henry would get that pound, not him. And how? Simple. He would trick the Tooth Fairy.

The house was quiet. Henry tip-toed into Peter's room. There was Peter, sound asleep, a big smile on his face. Henry sneaked his hand under Peter's pillow and stole the tooth.

Tee hee, thought Henry. He tiptoed out of Peter's room and bumped into Mum.

"AAAAGGGHH!" shrieked Henry.

"AAAAGGGHH!" shrieked Mum.

"You scared me," said Henry.

"What are you doing?" said Mum.

"Nothing," said Henry. "I thought I heard a noise in Peter's room and went to check."

Mum looked at Henry. Henry tried to look sweet.

"Go back to bed, Henry," said Mum.

Henry scampered to his room and put the tooth under his pillow. Phew. That was a close call. Henry smiled. Wouldn't

that cry-baby Peter be furious the next
morning when he found no tooth and no
money?

Henry woke up and felt under his pillow.
The tooth was gone. Hurray, thought
Henry. Now for the money.

Henry searched under the pillow.

Henry searched on top of the pillow. He searched under the covers, under Teddy, under the bed, everywhere. There was no money.

Henry heard Peter's footsteps pounding down the hall.

"Mum, Dad, look," said Peter. "A whole pound from the Tooth Fairy!"

"Great!" said Mum.

"Wonderful!" said Dad.

What?! thought Henry.

"Shall I share it with you, Mum?" said Peter.

"Thank you, darling Peter, but no thanks," said Mum. "It's for you."

"I'll have it," said Henry. "There are loads of comics I want to buy. And some –"

"No," said Peter. "It's mine. Get your own tooth."

Henry stared at his brother. Peter would never have dared to speak to him like that before.

Horrid Henry pretended he was a pirate captain pushing a prisoner off the plank.

"OWWW!" shrieked Peter.

"Don't be horrid, Henry," said Dad.

Henry decided to change the subject fast.

"Mum," said Henry. "How does the Tooth Fairy *know* who's lost a tooth?"

"She looks under the pillow," said Mum.

"But how does she know whose pillow to look under?"

"She just does," said Mum. "By magic."

"But how?" said Henry.

"She sees the gap between your teeth," said Mum.

Aha, thought Henry. That's where he'd gone wrong.

That night Henry cut out a small piece of black paper, wet it, and covered over his two bottom teeth. He smiled at himself in the mirror. Perfect, thought Henry. He smiled again.

Then Henry stuck a pair of dracula

teeth under his pillow. He tied a string round the biggest tooth, and tied the string to his finger. When the Tooth Fairy came, the string would pull on his finger and wake him up.

All right, Tooth Fairy, thought Henry. You think you're so smart. Find your way out of this one.

The next morning was Saturday. Henry woke up and felt under his pillow. The string was still attached to his finger, but the dracula teeth were gone. In their place was something small and round . . .

"My pound coin!" crowed Henry. He grabbed it.

The pound coin was plastic.

There must be some mistake, thought Henry. He checked under the pillow again. But all he found was a folded piece

214

of bright blue paper, covered in stars.

Henry opened it. There, in tiny gold letters, he read:

Nice try Henry

The Tooth Fairy

"Rats," said Henry.

From downstairs came the sound of Mum shouting.

"Henry! Get down here this minute!"

"What now?" muttered Henry, heaving his heavy bones out of bed.

"Yeah?" said Henry.

Mum held up an empty jar.

"Well?" said Mum.

Henry had forgotten all about the sweets.

"It wasn't me," said Henry automatically. "We must have mice."

"No sweets for a month," said Mum. "You'll eat apples instead. You can start right now."

Ugh. Apples. Henry hated all fruits and vegetables, but apples were the worst.

"Oh no," said Henry.

"Oh yes," said Mum. "Right now."

Henry took the apple and bit off the teeniest, tiniest piece he could.

CRUNCH. CRACK.

Henry choked. Then he swallowed, gasping and spluttering.

His mouth felt funny. Henry poked around with his tongue and felt a space.

He shoved his fingers in his mouth,
then ran to the mirror.

His tooth was gone.

He'd swallowed it.

"It's not fair!" shrieked Horrid Henry.

2

HORRID HENRY'S WEDDING

"I'm not wearing these horrible clothes and that's that!"

Horrid Henry glared at the mirror. A stranger smothered in a lilac ruffled shirt, green satin knickerbockers, tights, pink cummerbund tied in a floppy bow and pointy white satin shoes with gold buckles glared back at him.

Henry had never seen anyone looking so silly in his life.

"Aha ha ha ha ha!" shrieked Horrid Henry, pointing at the mirror.

Then Henry peered more closely. The ridiculous looking boy was him.

Perfect Peter stood next to Horrid Henry. He too was smothered in a lilac ruffled shirt, green satin knickerbockers, tights, pink cummerbund and pointy white shoes with gold buckles. But, unlike Henry, Peter was smiling.

"Aren't they adorable!" squealed Prissy Polly. "That's how my children are always going to dress."

Prissy Polly was Horrid Henry's horrible older cousin. Prissy Polly was always squeaking and squealing:

"Eeek, it's a speck of dust."

"Eeek, it's a puddle."

"Eeek, my hair is a mess."

But when Prissy Polly announced she was getting married to Pimply Paul and wanted Henry and Peter to be pageboys, Mum said yes before Henry could stop her.

"What's a pageboy?" asked Henry suspiciously.

"A pageboy carries the wedding rings down the aisle on a satin cushion," said Mum.

"And throws confetti afterwards," said Dad.

Henry liked the idea of throwing confetti. But carrying rings on a cushion? No thanks.

"I don't want to be a pageboy," said Henry.

"I do, I do," said Peter.

"You're going to be a pageboy, and that's that," said Mum.

"And you'll behave yourself," said Dad. "It's very kind of cousin Polly to ask you."

Henry scowled.

"Who'd want to be married to *her*?" said Henry. "I wouldn't if you paid me a

221

million pounds."

But for some reason the bridegroom, Pimply Paul, did want to marry Prissy Polly. And, as far as Henry knew, he had not been paid one million pounds.

Pimply Paul was also trying on his wedding clothes. He looked ridiculous in a black top hat, lilac shirt, and a black jacket covered in gold swirls.

"I won't wear these silly clothes," said Henry.

"Oh be quiet, you little brat," snapped Pimply Paul.

Horrid Henry glared at him.

"I won't," said Henry. "And that's final."

"Henry, stop being horrid," said Mum. She looked extremely silly in a big floppy hat dripping with flowers.

Suddenly Henry grabbed at the lace ruffles round his throat.

"I'm choking," he gasped. "I can't breathe."

Then Henry fell to the floor and rolled around.

"Ugggggghhhhhhh," moaned Henry. "I'm dying."

"Get up this minute, Henry!" said Dad.

"Eeek, there's dirt on the floor!" shrieked Polly.

"Can't you control that child?" hissed Pimply Paul.

"I DON'T WANT TO BE A PAGEBOY!" howled Horrid Henry.

"Thank you so much for asking me to be a pageboy, Polly," shouted Perfect Peter, trying to be heard over Henry's screams.

"You're welcome," shouted Polly.

"Stop that, Henry!" ordered Mum. "I've never been so ashamed in my life."

"I hate children," muttered Pimply Paul under his breath.

Horrid Henry stopped. Unfortunately, his pageboy clothes looked as fresh and crisp as ever.

All right, thought Horrid Henry. You want me at this wedding? You've got me.

Prissy Polly's wedding day arrived. Henry

was delighted to see rain pouring down. How cross Polly would be.

Perfect Peter was already dressed.

"Isn't this going to be fun, Henry?" said Peter.

"No!" said Henry, sitting on the floor. "And I'm not going."

Mum and Dad stuffed Henry into his pageboy clothes. It was hard, heavy work.

Finally everyone was in the car.

"We're going to be late!" shrieked Mum.

"We're going to be late!" shrieked Dad.

"We're going to be late!" shrieked Peter.

"Good!" muttered Henry.

Mum, Dad, Henry and Peter arrived at the church. Boom! There was a clap of thunder. Rain poured down. All the other guests were already inside.

"Watch out for the puddle, boys," said Mum, as she leapt out of the car. She opened her umbrella.

Dad jumped over the puddle.

Peter jumped over the puddle.

Henry jumped over the puddle, and tripped.

SPLASH!

"Oopsy," said Henry.

His ruffles were torn, his knickerbockers were filthy, and his satin shoes were soaked.

Mum, Dad, and Peter were covered in muddy water.

Perfect Peter burst into tears.

"You've ruined my pageboy clothes," sobbed Peter.

Mum wiped as much dirt as she could off Henry and Peter.

"It was an accident, Mum, really," said Henry.

"Hurry up, you're late!" shouted Pimply Paul.

Mum and Dad dashed into the church. Henry and Peter stayed outside, waiting to make their entrance.

Pimply Paul and his best man, Cross Colin, stared at Henry and Peter.

"You look a mess," said Paul.

"It was an accident," said Henry.

Peter snivelled.

"Now be careful with the wedding rings," said Cross Colin. He handed

Henry and Peter a satin cushion each,
with a gold ring on top.

A great quivering clump of lace and
taffeta and bows and flowers approached.
Henry guessed Prissy Polly must be
lurking somewhere underneath.

"Eeek," squeaked the clump. "Why
did it have to rain on my wedding?"

"Eeek," squeaked the clump again.
"You're filthy."

Perfect Peter began to sob. The satin
cushion trembled in his hand. The ring
balanced precariously near the edge.

Cross Colin snatched Peter's cushion.

"You can't carry a ring with your hand
shaking like that," snapped Colin.
"You'd better carry them both, Henry."

"Come *on*," hissed Pimply Paul.
"We're late!"

Cross Colin and Pimply Paul dashed
into the church.

The music started. Henry pranced down the aisle after Polly. Everyone stood up.

Henry beamed and bowed and waved. He was King Henry the Horrible, smiling graciously at his cheering subjects before he chopped off their heads.

As he danced along, he stepped on Polly's long, trailing dress.

Riiiiip.

"Eeeeek!" squeaked Prissy Polly.

Part of Polly's train lay beneath Henry's muddy satin shoe.

That dress was too long anyway, thought Henry. He kicked the fabric out of the way and stomped down the aisle.

The bride, groom, best man, and pageboys assembled in front of the minister.

Henry stood . . . and stood . . . and stood. The minister droned on . . . and

on . . . and on. Henry's arm holding up
the cushion began to ache.

This is boring, thought Henry, jiggling
the rings on the cushion.

Boing! Boing! Boing!

Oooh, thought Henry. I'm good at
ring tossing.

The rings bounced.

The minister droned.

Henry was a famous pancake chef,
tossing the pancakes higher and higher
and higher . . .

Clink clunk.

The rings rolled down the aisle and
vanished down a small grate.

Oops, thought Henry.

"May I have the rings, please?" said the
minister.

Everyone looked at Henry.

"He's got them," said Henry
desperately, pointing at Peter.

"I have not," sobbed Peter.

Henry reached into his pocket. He found two pieces of old chewing-gum, some gravel, and his lucky pirate ring.

"Here, use this," he said.

At last, Pimply Paul and Prissy Polly were married.

Cross Colin handed Henry and Peter a basket of pink and yellow rose petals each.

"Throw the petals in front of the bride and groom as they walk back down the aisle," whispered Colin.

"I will," said Peter. He scattered the petals before Pimply Paul and Prissy Polly.

"So will I," said Henry. He hurled a handful of petals in Pimply Paul's face.

"Watch it, you little brat," snarled Paul.

"Windy, isn't it?" said Henry. He hurled another handful of petals at Polly.

"Eeek," squeaked Prissy Polly.

"Everyone outside for the photographs," said the photographer.

Horrid Henry loved having his picture

taken. He dashed out.

"Pictures of the bride and groom first," said the photographer.

Henry jumped in front.

Click.

Henry peeked from the side.

Click.

Henry stuck out his tongue.
Click.
Henry made horrible rude faces.
Click.

"This way to the reception!" said
Cross Colin.

The wedding party was held in a nearby hotel.

The adults did nothing but talk and eat, talk and drink, talk and eat.

Perfect Peter sat at the table and ate his lunch.

Horrid Henry sat under the table and poked people's legs. He crawled around and squashed some toes. Then Henry got bored and drifted into the next room.

There was the wedding cake, standing alone, on a little table. It was the most beautiful, delicious-looking cake Henry had ever seen. It had three layers and was covered in luscious white icing and yummy iced flowers and bells and leaves.

Henry's mouth watered.

I'll just taste a teeny weeny bit of petal, thought Henry. No harm in that.

He broke off a morsel and popped it in his mouth.

Hmmmm boy! That icing tasted great.

Perhaps just one more bite, thought Henry. If I take it from the back, no one will notice.

Henry carefully selected an icing rose from the bottom tier and stuffed it in his mouth. Wow.

Henry stood back from the cake. It looked a little uneven now, with that rose missing from the bottom.

I'll just even it up, thought Henry. It was the work of a moment to break off a rose from the middle tier and another from the top.

Then a strange thing happened.

"Eat me," whispered the cake. "Go on."

Who was Henry to ignore such a request?

He picked out a few crumbs from the back.

Delicious, thought Henry. Then he took a few more. And a few more. Then he dug out a nice big chunk.

"What do you think you're doing?" shouted Pimply Paul.

Henry ran round the cake table. Paul ran after him.

Round and round and round the cake they ran.

"Just wait till I get my hands on you!" snarled Pimply Paul.

237

Henry dashed under the table.

Pimply Paul lunged for him and missed.

SPLAT.

Pimply Paul fell head first on to the cake.

Henry slipped away.

Prissy Polly ran into the room.

"Eeek," she shrieked.

"Wasn't that a lovely wedding," sighed Mum on the way home. "Funny they didn't have a cake, though."

"Oh yes," said Dad.

"Oh yes," said Peter.

"OH YES!" said Henry. "I'll be glad to be a pageboy anytime."

3

MOODY MARGARET MOVES IN

Mum was on the phone.

"Of course we'd be delighted to have Margaret," she said. "It will be no trouble at all."

Henry stopped breaking the tails off Peter's plastic horses.

"WHAT?" he howled.

"Shh, Henry," said Mum. "No, no," she added. "Henry is delighted, too. See you Friday."

"What's going on?" said Henry.

"Margaret is coming to stay while her

parents go on holiday," said Mum.

Henry was speechless with horror.

"She's going to stay . . . here?"

"Yes," said Mum.

"How long?" said Henry.

"Two weeks," said Mum brightly.

Horrid Henry could not stand Moody
Margaret for more than two minutes.

"Two weeks?" he said. "I'll run away!
I'll lock her out of the house, I'll pull her
hair out, I'll . . ."

"Don't be horrid, Henry," said Mum.
"Margaret's a lovely girl and I'm sure
we'll have fun."

"No we won't," said Henry. "Not
with that moody old grouch."

"I'll have fun," said Perfect Peter. "I
love having guests."

"She's not sleeping in my room," said
Horrid Henry. "She can sleep in the
cellar."

"No," said Mum. "You'll move into Peter's room and let Margaret have your bed."

Horrid Henry opened his mouth to scream, but only a rasping sound came out. He was so appalled he could only gasp.

"Give . . . up . . . my . . . room!" he choked. "To . . . Margaret?"

Margaret spying on *his* treasures, sleeping in *his* bed, playing with *his* toys while he had to share a room with Peter . . .

"No!" howled Henry. He fell on the floor and screamed. "NO!!"

"I don't mind giving up my bed for a guest," said Perfect Peter. "It's the polite thing to do. Guests come first."

Henry stopped howling just long enough to kick Peter.

"Owww!" screamed Peter. He burst

into tears, "Mum!"

"Henry!" yelled Mum. "You horrid boy! Say sorry to Peter."

"She's not coming!" shrieked Henry. "And that's final."

"Go to your room!" yelled Mum.

Moody Margaret arrived at Henry's house with her parents, four suitcases, seven boxes of toys, two pillows, and a trumpet.

"Margaret won't be any trouble," said her mum. "She's always polite, eats everything, and never complains. Isn't that right, Precious?"

"Yes," said Margaret.

"Margaret's no fusspot," said her dad. "She's good as gold, aren't you, Precious?"

"Yes," said Margaret.

"Have a lovely holiday," said Mum.

"We will," said Margaret's parents.

The door slammed behind them.

Moody Margaret marched into the sitting room and swept a finger across the mantelpiece.

"It's not very clean, is it?" she said. "You'd never find so much dust at *my* house."

"Oh," said Dad.

"A little dust never hurt anyone," said Mum.

"I'm allergic," said Margaret. "One whiff of dust and I start to . . . sn . . . sn . . . ACHOOO!" she sneezed.

"We'll clean up right away," said Mum.

Dad mopped.

Mum swept.

Peter dusted.

Henry hoovered.

Margaret directed.

"Henry, you've missed a big dust-ball right there," said Margaret, pointing under the sofa.

Horrid Henry hoovered as far away from the dust as possible.

"Not there, here!" said Margaret.

Henry aimed the hoover at Margaret. He was a fire-breathing dragon burning his prey to a crisp.

"Help!" shrieked Margaret.

"Henry!" said Dad.

"Don't be horrid," said Mum.

"I think Henry should be punished," said Margaret. "I think he should be locked in his bedroom for three weeks."

"I don't have a bedroom to be locked up in 'cause you're in it," said Henry. He glared at Margaret.

Margaret glared back.

"I'm the guest, Henry, so you'd better be polite," hissed Margaret.

"Of course he'll be polite," said Mum. "Don't worry, Margaret. Any trouble, you come straight to me."

"Thank you," said Moody Margaret, smiling. "I will. I'm hungry," she added. "Why isn't supper ready?"

"It will be soon," said Dad.

"But I *always* eat at six o'clock," said Margaret, "I want to eat NOW."

"All right," said Dad.

Horrid Henry and Moody Margaret dashed for the seat facing the garden. Margaret got there first. Henry shoved her off. Then Margaret shoved him off.

Thud. Henry landed on the floor.

"Ouch," said Henry.

"Let the guest have the chair," said Dad.

"But that's *my* chair," said Henry. "That's where I *always* sit."

"Have my chair, Margaret," said Perfect Peter. "I don't mind."

"I want to sit here," said Moody Margaret. "I'm the guest so *I* decide."

Horrid Henry dragged himself around the table and sat next to Peter.

"OUCH!" shrieked Margaret. "Henry kicked me!"

"No I didn't," said Henry, outraged.

"Stop it, Henry," said Mum. "That's no way to treat a guest."

Henry stuck out his tongue at Margaret. Moody Margaret stuck out her tongue even further, then stomped on his foot.

"OUCH!" shrieked Henry. "Margaret kicked me!"

Moody Margaret gasped. "Oh I'm ever

so sorry, Henry," she said sweetly. "It was an accident. Silly me. I didn't mean to, really I didn't."

Dad brought the food to the table.

"What's *that*?" asked Margaret.

"Baked beans, corn on the cob, and chicken," said Dad.

"I don't like baked beans," said Margaret. "And I like my corn *off* the cob."

Mum scraped the corn off the cob.

"No, put the corn on a separate plate!" shrieked Margaret. "I don't like vegetables touching my meat."

Dad got out the pirate plate, the duck plate, and the "Happy birthday Peter" plate.

"I want the pirate plate," said Margaret, snatching it.

"I want the pirate plate," said Henry, snatching it back.

"I don't mind which plate I get," said Perfect Peter. "A plate's a plate."

"No it isn't!" shouted Henry.

"I'm the guest," shouted Margaret. "I get to choose."

"Give her the pirate plate, Henry," said Dad.

"It's not fair," said Henry, glaring at his plate decorated with little ducks.

"She's the guest," said Mum.

"So?" said Henry. Wasn't there an ancient Greek who stretched all his guests on an iron bed if they were too short or lopped off their heads and feet if they were too long? That guy sure knew how to deal with horrible guests like Moody Margaret.

"Yuck," said Margaret, spitting out a mouthful of chicken. "You've put salt on it!"

"Only a little," said Dad.

"I never eat salt," said Moody
Margaret. "It's not good for me. And I
always have peas at *my* house."

"We'll get some tomorrow," said
Mum.

Peter lay asleep in the top bunk. Horrid Henry sat listening by the door. He'd scattered crumbs all over Margaret's bed. He couldn't wait to hear her scream.

But there wasn't a sound coming from Henry's room, where Margaret the invader lay. Henry couldn't understand it.

Sadly, he climbed into (oh, the shame of it) the *bottom* bunk. Then he screamed. His bed was filled with jam, crumbs, and something squishy squashy and horrible.

"Go to sleep, Henry!" shouted Dad.

That Margaret! He'd booby-trap the room, cut up her doll's clothes, paint her face purple . . . Henry smiled grimly. Oh yes, he'd fix Moody Margaret.

Mum and Dad sat in the sitting room watching TV.

Moody Margaret appeared on the stairs.

"I can't sleep with that noise," she said.

Mum and Dad looked at each other.

"We are watching very quietly, dear," said Mum.

"But I can't sleep if there's any noise in the house," said Margaret. "I have very sensitive ears."

Mum turned off the TV and picked up her knitting needles.

Click click click.

Margaret reappeared.

"I can't sleep with that clicking noise," she said.

"All right," said Mum. She sighed a little.

"And it's cold in my bedroom," said Moody Margaret.

Mum turned up the heat.

Margaret reappeared.

"Now it's too hot," said Moody Margaret.

Dad turned down the heat.

"My room smells funny," said Margaret.

"My bed is too hard," said Margaret.

"My room is too stuffy," said Margaret.

"My room is too light," said Margaret.

"Goodnight, Margaret," said Mum.

"How many more days is she staying?" said Dad.

Mum looked at the calendar.

"Only thirteen," said Mum.

Dad hid his face in his hands.

"I don't know if I can live that long," said Dad.

TOOTA TOOT. Mum blasted out of bed.

TOOTA TOOT. Dad blasted out of bed.

TOOTA TOOT. TOOTA TOOT.

TOOTA TOOT TOOT TOOT. Henry
and Peter blasted out of bed.

Margaret marched down the hall,
playing her trumpet.

TOOTA TOOT. TOOTA TOOT.

TOOTA TOOT TOOT TOOT
TOOT.

"Margaret, would you mind playing
your trumpet a little later?" said Dad,
clutching his ears. "It's six o'clock in the
morning."

"That's when I wake up," said
Margaret.

"Could you play a little more softly?"
said Mum.

"But I have to practise," said Moody
Margaret.

The trumpet blared through the house.
TOOT TOOT TOOT.

Horrid Henry turned on his boom
box.

BOOM BOOM BOOM.

Margaret played her trumpet louder.
TOOT! TOOT! TOOT!

Henry blasted his boom box as loud as
he could.

BOOM! BOOM! BOOM!

"Henry!" shrieked Mum.

"Turn that down!" bellowed Dad.

"Quiet!" screamed Margaret. "I can't practise with all this noise." She put down her trumpet. "And I'm hungry. Where's my breakfast?"

"We have breakfast at eight," said Mum.

"But I want breakfast now," said Margaret.

Mum had had enough.

"No," said Mum firmly. "We eat at eight."

Margaret opened her mouth and screamed. No one could scream as long, or as loud, as Moody Margaret.

Her piercing screams echoed through the house.

"All right," said Mum. She knew when she was beaten. "We'll eat now."

Henry's diary.

Monday I put crumbs in Margaret's bed. She put jam, crusts and slugs in mine.

Tuesday Margaret found my secret biscuits and crisps and ate every single one.

Wednesday I can't play tapes at night because it disturbs grumpy-face Margaret.

Thursday I can't sing because it disturbs frog-face.

Friday I can't breathe because it disturbs misery-guts.

Saturday I can stand it No Longer

That night, when everyone was asleep, Horrid Henry crept into the sitting room and picked up the phone.

"I'd like to leave a message," he whispered.

Bang bang bang bang bang.

Ding dong! Ding dong! Ding dong!

Henry sat up in bed.

Someone was banging on the front door and ringing the bell.

"Who could that be at this time of night?" yawned Mum.

Dad peeked through the window then opened the door.

"Where's my baby?" shouted Margaret's mum.

"Where's my baby?" shouted Margaret's dad.

"Upstairs," said Mum. "Where else?"

"What's happened to her?" shrieked Margaret's mum.

"We got here as quick as we could!" shrieked Margaret's dad.

Mum and Dad looked at each other. What was going on?

"She's fine," said Mum.

Margaret's mum and dad looked at each other. What was going on?

"But the message said it was an emergency and to come at once," said Margaret's mum.

"We cut short our holiday," said Margaret's dad.

"What message?" said Mum.

"What's going on? I can't sleep with all this noise," said Moody Margaret.

Margaret and her parents had gone home.

"What a terrible mix-up," said Mum.

"Such a shame they cut short their holiday," said Dad.

"Still . . ." said Mum. She looked at Dad.

"Hmmn," said Dad.

"You don't think that Henry . . ." said Mum.

"Not even Henry could do something so horrid," said Dad.

Mum frowned.

"Henry!" said Mum.

Henry continued sticking Peter's stamps together.

"Yeah?"

"Do you know anything about a message?"

"Me?" said Henry.

"You," said Mum.

"No," said Henry. "It's a mystery."

"That's a lie, Henry," said Perfect Peter.

"Is not," said Henry.

"Is too," said Peter. "I heard you on the phone."

Henry lunged at Peter. He was a mad bull charging the matador.

"YOWWWWW," shrieked Peter.

Henry stopped. He was in for it now. No pocket money for a year. No sweets for ten years. No TV ever.

Henry squared his shoulders and waited for his punishment.

Dad put his feet up.

"That was a terrible thing to do," said Dad.

Mum turned on the TV.

"Go to your room," said Mum.

Henry bounced upstairs. Your room. Sweeter words were never spoken.

4

HORRID HENRY'S NEW TEACHER

"Now Henry," said Dad. "Today is the first day of school. A chance for a fresh start with a new teacher."

"Yeah, yeah," scowled Horrid Henry.

He hated the first day of term. Another year, another teacher to show who was boss. His first teacher, Miss Marvel, had run screaming from the classroom after two weeks. His next teacher, Mrs Zip, had run screaming from the classroom after one day. Breaking in new teachers wasn't easy, thought Henry, but someone had to do it.

Dad got out a piece of paper and waved it.

"Henry, I never want to read another school report like this again," he said. "Why can't your school reports be like Peter's?"

Henry started whistling.

"Pay attention, Henry," shouted Dad. "This is important. Look at this report."

HENRY'S SCHOOL REPORT

It has been horrible Teaching Henry this year. He is rude, lazy and disruptive. The worst student I have ever taught.

Behaviour: Horrid

English: Horrid

Maths: Horrid

Science: Horrid

P.E: Horrid

"What about *my* report?" said Perfect
Peter.

Dad beamed.

"Your report was perfect, Peter," said
Dad. "Keep up the wonderful work."

PETER'S SCHOOL REPORT

It has been a pleasure
teaching Peter this year. He is
polite, hard-working and
co-operative. The best student I
have ever taught.

Behaviour: Perfect

English: Perfect

Maths: Perfect

Science: Perfect

P.E: Perfect

Peter smiled proudly.

"You'll just have to try harder,
Henry," said Peter, smirking.

Horrid Henry was a shark sinking his teeth into a drowning sailor.

"OWWWW," shrieked Peter. "Henry bit me!"

"Don't be horrid, Henry!" shouted Dad. "Or no TV for a week."

"I don't care," muttered Henry. When he became King he'd make it a law that parents, not children, had to go to school.

Horrid Henry pushed and shoved his way into class and grabbed the seat next to Rude Ralph.

"Nah nah ne nah nah, I've got a new football," said Ralph.

Henry didn't have a football. He'd kicked his through Moody Margaret's window.

"Who cares?" said Horrid Henry.

The classroom door slammed. It was

Mr Nerdon, the toughest, meanest, nastiest teacher in the school.

"SILENCE!" he said, glaring at them with his bulging eyes. "I don't want to hear a sound. I don't even want to hear anyone breathe."

The class held its breath.

"GOOD!" he growled. "I'm Mr Nerdon."

Henry snorted. What a stupid name.

"Nerd," he whispered to Ralph.

Rude Ralph giggled.

"Nerdy Nerd," whispered Horrid Henry, snickering.

Mr Nerdon walked up to Henry and jabbed his finger in his face.

"Quiet, you horrible boy!" said Mr Nerdon. "I've got my eye on you. Oh yes. I've heard about your other teachers. Bah! I'm made of stronger stuff. There will be no nonsense in *my* class."

We'll see about that, thought Henry.

"Our first sums for the year are on the board. Now get to work," ordered Mr Nerdon.

Horrid Henry had an idea.

Quickly he scribbled a note to Ralph.

Ralph – I bet you that I can make Mr. Nerdon run screaming out of class by the end of lunchtime.

No way, Henry

If I do will you give me your new football?

O.K. But if you don't, you have to give me your pound coin.

O.K.

Horrid Henry took a deep breath and went to work. He rolled up some paper, stuffed it in his mouth, and spat it out. The spitball whizzed through the air and pinged Mr Nerdon on the back of his neck.

Mr Nerdon wheeled round.

"You!" snapped Mr Nerdon. "Don't you mess with me!"

"It wasn't *me*!" said Henry. "It was Ralph."

"Liar!" said Mr Nerdon. "Sit at the back of the class."

Horrid Henry moved his seat next to Clever Clare.

"Move over, Henry!" hissed Clare. "You're on my side of the desk."

Henry shoved her.

"Move over yourself," he hissed back.

Then Horrid Henry reached over and broke Clare's pencil.

"Henry broke my pencil!" shrieked Clare.

Mr Nerdon moved Henry next to Weepy William.

Henry pinched him.

Mr Nerdon moved Henry next to Tough Toby.

Henry jiggled the desk.

Mr Nerdon moved Henry next to Lazy Linda.

Henry scribbled all over her paper.

Mr Nerdon moved Henry next to Moody Margaret.

Moody Margaret drew a line down the middle of the desk.

"Cross that line, Henry, and you're dead," said Margaret under her breath.

Henry looked up. Mr Nerdon was writing spelling words on the board.

Henry started to rub out Margaret's line.

"Stop it, Henry," said Mr Nerdon, without turning round.

Henry stopped.

Mr Nerdon continued writing.

Henry pulled Margaret's hair.

Mr Nerdon moved Henry next to Beefy Bert, the biggest boy in the class.

Beefy Bert was chewing his pencil and trying to add 2 + 2 without much luck.

Horrid Henry inched his chair on to Beefy Bert's side of the desk.

Bert ignored him.

Henry poked him.

Bert ignored him.

Henry hit him.

POW!

The next thing Henry knew he was lying on the floor, looking up at the ceiling. Beefy Bert continued chewing his pencil.

"What happened, Bert?" said Mr Nerdon.

"I dunno," said Beefy Bert.

"Get up off the floor, Henry!" said Mr Nerdon. A faint smile appeared on the teacher's slimy lips.

"He hit me!" said Henry. He'd never

felt such a punch in his life.

"It was an accident," said Mr Nerdon. He smirked. "You'll sit next to Bert from now on."

That's it, thought Henry. Now it's war.

"How absurd, to be a nerdy bird," said Horrid Henry behind Mr Nerdon's back.

Slowly Mr Nerdon turned and walked towards him. His hand was clenched into a fist.

"Since you're so good at rhyming," said Mr Nerdon. "Everyone write a poem. Now."

Henry slumped in his seat and groaned. A poem! Yuck! He hated poems. Even the word *poem* made him want to throw up.

Horrid Henry caught Rude Ralph's eye. Ralph was grinning and mouthing, "A pound, a pound!" at him. Time was running out. Despite Henry's best efforts, Mr Nerdon still hadn't run screaming from the class. Henry would have to act fast to get that football.

What horrible poem could he write? Horrid Henry smiled. Quickly he picked up his pencil and went to work.

"Now, who's my first victim?" said Mr Nerdon. He looked round the room. "Susan! Read your poem."

Sour Susan stood up and read:

> "Bow wow
> Bow wow
> Woof woof woof
> I'm a dog, not a cat, so . . .
> SCAT!"

"Not enough rhymes," said Mr

Nerdon. "Next . . ." He looked round the room. "Graham!"

Greedy Graham stood up and read:

"Chocolate chocolate chocolate sweet,
Cakes and doughnuts can't be beat.
Ice cream is my favourite treat
With lots and lots of pie to eat!"

"Too many rhymes," said Mr Nerdon. "Next . . ." He scowled at the class. Henry tried to look as if he didn't want the teacher to call on him.

"Henry!" snapped Mr Nerdon. "Read your poem!"

Horrid Henry stood up and read:

"Pirates puke on stormy seas,
Giants spew on top of trees."

Henry peeked at Mr Nerdon. He
looked pale. Henry continued to read:

"Kings are sick in golden loos,
Dogs throw up on Daddy's shoes."

Henry peeked again at Mr Nerdon. He
looked green. Any minute now, thought
Henry, and he'll be out of here
screaming. He read on:

"Babies love to make a mess,
Down the front of Mum's best dress.

279

And what car ride would be complete,
Without the stink of last night's treat?"

"That's enough," choked Mr Nerdon.

"Wait, I haven't got to the good bit," said Horrid Henry.

"I said that's enough!" gasped Mr Nerdon. "You fail."

He made a big black mark in his book.

"I threw up on the boat!" shouted Greedy Graham.

"I threw up on the plane!" shouted Sour Susan.

"I threw up in the car!" shouted Dizzy Dave.

"I said that's enough!" ordered Mr Nerdon. He glared at Horrid Henry. "Get out of here, all of you! It's lunchtime."

Rats, thought Henry. Mr Nerdon was one tough teacher.

280

Rude Ralph grabbed him.

"Ha ha, Henry," said Ralph. "You lose. Gimme that pound."

"No," said Henry. "I've got until the end of lunch."

"You can't do anything to him between now and then," said Ralph.

"Oh yeah?" said Henry. "Just watch me."

Then Henry had a wonderful, spectacular idea. This was it. The best plan he'd ever had. Someday someone would stick a plaque on the school wall celebrating Henry's genius. There would be songs written about him. He'd probably even get a medal. But first things first. In order for his plan to work to perfection, he needed Peter.

Perfect Peter was playing hopscotch with his friends Tidy Ted and Spotless Sam.

"Hey Peter," said Henry. "How would you like to be a real member of the Purple Hand?"

The Purple Hand was Horrid Henry's secret club. Peter had wanted to join for ages, but naturally Henry would never let him.

Peter's jaw dropped open.

"Me?" said Peter.

"Yes," said Henry. "If you can pass the secret club test."

"What do I have to do?" said Peter eagerly.

"It's tricky," said Henry. "And probably much too hard for you."

"Tell me, tell me," said Peter.

"All you have to do is lie down right there below that window and stay absolutely still. You mustn't move until I tell you to."

"Why?" said Peter.

"Because that's the test," said Henry.

Perfect Peter thought for a moment.

"Are you going to drop something on me?"

"No," said Henry.

"OK," said Peter. He lay down obediently.

"And I need your shoes," said Henry.

"Why?" said Peter.

Henry scowled.

"Do you want to be in the secret club or not?" said Henry.

"I do," said Peter.

"Then give me your shoes and be quiet," said Henry. "I'll be checking on you. If I see you moving one little bit you can't be in my club."

Peter gave Henry his trainers, then lay still as a statue.

Horrid Henry grabbed the shoes, then dashed up the stairs to his classroom.

It was empty. Good.

Horrid Henry went over to the window and opened it. Then he stood there, holding one of Peter's shoes in each hand.

Henry waited until he heard Mr Nerdon's footsteps. Then he went into action.

"Help!" shouted Horrid Henry. "Help!"

Mr Nerdon entered. He saw Henry and glowered.

"What are you doing here? Get out!"

"Help!" shouted Henry. "I can't hold on to him much longer . . . he's slipping . . . aaahhh, he's fallen!"

Horrid Henry held up the empty shoes.

"He's gone," whispered Henry. He peeked out of the window. "Ugghh, I can't look."

Mr Nerdon went pale. He ran to the window and saw Perfect Peter lying still and shoeless on the ground below.

"Oh no," gasped Mr Nerdon.

"I'm sorry," panted Henry. "I tried to hold on to him, honest, I – "

"Help!" screamed Mr Nerdon. He raced down the stairs. "Police! Fire! Ambulance! Help! Help!"

He ran over to Peter and knelt by his still body.

"Can I get up now, Henry?" said Perfect Peter.

"What!?" gasped Mr Nerdon. "What did you say?"

Then the terrible truth dawned. He, Ninius Nerdon, had been tricked.

"YOU HORRID BOY! GO STRAIGHT TO THE HEAD TEACHER – NOW!" screeched Mr Nerdon.

Perfect Peter jumped to his feet.

"But . . . but –" spluttered Perfect Peter.

"Now!" screamed Mr Nerdon. "How dare you! To the head!"

"AAAGGGHHHH," shrieked Peter.

He slunk off to the head's office, weeping.

Mr Nerdon turned to race up the stairs to grab Henry.

"I'll get you, Henry!" he screamed. His face was white. He looked as if he were going to faint.

"Help," squeaked Mr Nerdon.

Then he fainted.

Clunk! Thunk! Thud!

NEE NAW NEE NAW NEE NAW.

When the ambulance arrived, the only person lying on the ground was Mr Nerdon. They scooped him on to a stretcher and took him away.

The perfect end to a perfect day, thought Horrid Henry, throwing his new football in the air. Peter sent home in disgrace. Mr Nerdon gone for good. Even the news that scary Miss Battle-Axe would be teaching Henry's class didn't bother him. After all, tomorrow was another day.